DEVIL WIND

A Clay Jared Western

R. Annan

Devil Wind
Copyright 2015 R. Annan
Edition 1.1
WGA Reg. #R31666

Photography © L. Annan
Editor: Karren Doll Tolliver

One Vision Publishing
ISBN: 978-1-942338-46-8 (eBook)
ISBN: 978-1-942338-45-1 (Print)

Western books by R. Annan:

Fight for The Lazy M
The Gunfighter in Winter
Long Ride to Hell's Kitchen
Owl Hawks
Gunfight at Barfield Springs
Shootout at Sanctuary City
Last Days of a Gunfighter
Copperhead Moon
Cowboys of the Box R
Prisoners of Brimstone Pass
Range War in C Minor

Dedication

To

Karren Doll Tolliver (a.k.a. 2Rs)

1.

Young Virgil McClain and Clay Jared met by chance at the Walnut River in the Kansas outback. The riverbed was so dry and hard an elephant could walk across it without making a dent.

Both men needed to water their horses.

McClain was dressed from head to toe in the traditional black clothing of a professional gunfighter. This pegged him as a fast-draw artist, a gun for hire. His wide-brimmed hat, shirt, pants and boots were offset by a brown cowhide vest. The vest, boots and brim of the hat were adorned with Mexican conches and yellow chamois strips.

Virgil McClain was a sight to behold.

In addition to his attractive clothes, McClain's face was handsome as well. He had black hair, greenish-gray eyes, a straight nose and a perfect mouth. He also sported a mustache above his upper lip that gave him a rakish, daring look.

He wore a single-action Colt on his right hip. Jared judged him to be young, in his twenties maybe. Jared himself was thirty-five, although he looked a little older. He pretty much had a seasoned, weathered look.

"Looks like we're out of luck. You got any water?"

Jared tossed his canteen over to McClain. The man took a drink and tossed it back.

"Thanks," he said. "I ran dry early yesterday."

"Where you headed, friend?" Jared asked.

"Ellsworth or Hays City. Haven't made up my mind. Right now I gotta get my pal here to water." He patted his horse's neck. "He's so dry he can't even take a piss."

Jared nodded. "Well, I'm headed north, myself." He nudged his horse into a slow walk. "So long." He had gone a few yards when McClain rode up alongside.

"Mind if I ride along? I'm headed north, too."

"Sure. My name is Jared. Clay Jared.

"I'm Virgil McClain," the gunslinger said. He reached across to shake Jared's hand.

They didn't say much after that. Their horses left a trail of curling dust behind.

As they rode along at a slow canter they saw visible signs of the drought. Scrub oaks stood bare on the parched, red earth and the switch grass lay bent and wilted. The July sun had sucked the moisture out of everything. The earth had surrendered to a stronger force.

"You play cards?" McClain asked.

"Some. Not much. You?"

McClain chuckled. "When I need money I do. I made a living with cardboard once." He sounded proud of the fact.

"Why did you quit?"

"Well, to be truthful, it always seemed like I was being accused of cheating."

Jared chuckled. "How did that go?"

"It always ended up with me putting a bullet in some dumb cowboy," McClain said. "No offense meant."

"None taken," Jared replied. After a moment he asked, "Did you?"

"Did I what?"

"Did you cheat?"

McClain laughed. "If I was being cheated on, yes."

They came over a rise and stopped to look down into a small valley. A white clapboard house with two levels stood out against the umber, ochre and sienna of the dry earth. There was a large red barn, a corral and a bunkhouse arranged in a U. A windmill stood by the corral, which had less than a dozen horses in it. There was a cistern pump in the yard by the house. A whitewashed wooden fence enclosed the compound.

"Let's see if they have water," McClain said.

Jared nodded. They walked their horses down the long slope through the open gate into the yard.

"Over there."

Jared pointed to a water trough by the windmill. The horses snorted and made for the trough without any urging. In a few seconds, they were sucking up the water.

McClain and Jared dismounted. They leaned over the trough and splashed water on their faces.

"Hold it!"

McClain whirled and went for his gun, then stopped. He wiped the water from his face, uncoiled and smiled.

Jared looked over at the porch where a young woman of about eighteen stood pointing a double-barreled shotgun at him and McClain. Although she was dressed like a man in shirt, pants and boots, she would never be mistaken for one.

Her hair was the color of autumn leaves when they turn orange-brown. Even from where she stood, in the shadow of the porch, Jared could see the purple in her eyes. Her skin had that pinkish, fresh-air look. She stood tall, straight, unafraid and beautiful.

"Afternoon, ma'am," McClain said in a voice meant to charm. He touched the brim of his hat in a salute. Jared watched as McClain walked a few steps towards the porch.

"Ma'am, please don't point that scattergun at me. It just might go off by accident."

An old man in a wheelchair came rolling out of the house, stopping beside the girl.

"What's wrong, Kim?"

"Nothin' I can't handle, Gran'paw," the girl said. She had a husky voice, raw like the wind.

The old man's hands were twisted with arthritis. His straggly white hair fell over his forehead, shielding his glaring, deep-set, dark eyes, eyes that blazed like burning coals. It was plain to see that he had once been a big, strong man of the West. But that was a long time ago. The Kansas plains had taken its toll on him.

"Who are you and whatta ya want!" he bellowed.

"My name is Virgil McClain, sir."

The dark, deep-set eyes bore into McClain's soul.

"Yer a gunslinger, aincha!"

"Ah, well, not exactly, sir," McClain back-pedaled. He walked slowly towards the porch, removing his hat.

"Well, yer dressed like a gunslinger an' that means Jorth sent ya ta kill us!" the old man yelled.

"Jorth?" McClain said. "I don't know anyone by that name, sir."

"Yer a lyin' polecat! Shoot 'em both, Kim!"

Jared walked up alongside McClain.

"Look," he explained, "we just stopped to water our horses. The Walnut River is bone-dry."

The girl stared at Jared for a moment.

"Where are you from, mister?"

She eyed McClain as she talked to Jared.

"South of here, ma'am. I last worked for the Compton spread, the Circle C. My name is Clay Jared."

"Clay Jared!" someone said loudly.

Jared looked around in surprise.

A cowboy with his right arm in a sling came out of the bunkhouse saying, "I'm Frank Selby. I was with the Flying W. A small spread east of the Circle C. Heck, man, yer a legend!" Selby looked at the girl. "He's alright, Miss Kim. He rides fer the brand, an' thet's fer sure!"

The woman called Kim lowered the barrel of her shotgun. She couldn't take her eyes off McClain. He stared boldly back at her, a wide smile on his face.

"I'm Kim Darnell," she said. "This is my grandfather, Seth."

"How do you do, Mrs. Darnell?" McClain said smoothly.

"I ain't a Mrs. I'm a Miss, Mr. McClain."

"Virgil, ma'am. Please. Just Virgil." The gunslinger turned to the old man. "How do you do, sir?"

Old Seth Darnell didn't return the courtesy. He grumbled and wheeled himself back into the house.

"Gran'paw isn't overly friendly," Kim Darnell said.

"So I see," McClain chuckled.

"Would you and yer friend like a cup of coffee, Mr. McClain?" Kim asked.

"We sure would, wouldn't we, Jared?" McClain replied.

"Yes, ma'am," Jared said.

"You, too, Frank," the girl said to Selby.

They went into the house through a hallway into the kitchen and sat down at a long, plank-board table.

The young girl leaned the shotgun in a corner and started making coffee at a huge cast-iron stove. A moment later they heard someone coming up the back porch steps into the storeroom behind the kitchen.

"We got company, Momma!" Kim said.

"I saw them come in." It was an older woman's voice.

Selby, Jared and McClain stood up as a woman carrying an empty wicker clothesbasket came in from the outside, bringing the smell of fresh air with her. It was hard to tell her age. She was a likeness of her daughter in every way, but more. Her beauty had been roughed out by time and experience.

"I'm Fran Darnell."

Jared and McClain introduced themselves.

Fran Darnell stared at McClain, slowly looking him up and down. She nodded.

"I see by your attire you're a gunslinger, Mr. McClain," she asserted bluntly, as if confirming a fact.

For a moment McClain was caught off-guard but quickly recovered.

"When the need arises, yes, ma'am," McClain replied.

"Are you for hire?"

The question really set McClain back on his heels. At a loss for words, he looked over at the young girl for a moment. "I guess I could be, ma'am."

"How much do you charge?"

Again, the gunslinger searched for words.

"That depends. What did you have in mind, Mrs. Darnell?"

"Killing a man is what I have in mind."

2.

"Mom!" Kim Darnell yelled, as if embarrassed.

"I usually deal with menfolk," McClain said after he recovered from surprise.

"My husband can't deal with anyone," Fran Darnell replied. "He's buried out back on the hill. Bill Jorth or his men killed him. It's all one and the same to me."

Kim cut in. "We don't know that fer sure, Mom."

"Who else could it be? You know Jorth and your father hated each other. They couldn't even stand the sight of one another."

"Who's this Jorth?" McClain asked.

"He owns the Circle J, east of the Diamond D," Fran answered.

"One of his men winged me a week ago," Selby said.

"Where did that happen?" Jared asked.

"Up at the east border, near the line shack."

"You get a good look at the shooter?"

"No, not really," Selby admitted.

"What makes you think it was one of Jorth's men?"

Selby shrugged. "Because his men have been ridin' over the east line an' stealin' Diamond D cattle."

"It was a Jorth man alright," Fran said with conviction.

"Not to be nosey but why was he shooting at you?"

"Because I caught him rustlin' a few Diamond D cows. We never did get those cows back." Selby sighed. "They probably got them branded over by now."

McClain wasn't listening. He didn't seem to be interested in the conversation at hand. His mind was on Kim Darnell. She seemed to be enjoying his attention.

Jared went on with his questions.

"How many head do you have, Mrs. Darnell?"

Selby answered before Fran Darnell could. "Not many. What ain't been stolen are dropping like flies for want of water."

Fran Darnell sat down at the table and faced Jared.

"We had ten thousand," she said. "All the streams running into Walnut Creek are dried up like it is. It hasn't rained here in the last two months. Like Frank says, the cattle are dropping like flies."

"How big is your spread?"

"The Diamond D is around twenty thousand acres, give or take a few. Why?"

"Seems like there ought to be water coming up underneath from someplace out there."

"I ain't seen any, an' I know jest about every inch of the spread," Selby said.

"What's north of the spread?" Jared asked.

"I don't really know," Fran replied.

"Nothin' but hills and rocks," Selby added. "It's government land. Unfit fer cows. Lots of locoweed. It ain't no place fer cows, that's fer sure."

"We're lucky to have what water we get pumped up by the windmill," Fran said. "And the cistern in the yard. If it doesn't rain soon, I'm afraid they'll give out, too."

Selby looked at Jared. "I guess you'll be movin' on?"

Jared shrugged. "I don't know. Maybe not. I might just stick around and look for a job. I've been drifting now for almost a month."

"You must be a bit saddle-weary, Mr. Jared," Fran said. "You're welcome to spend the night down in the bunkhouse, if you care to. It's all but empty. And you, too, Mr. McClain."

"I wouldn't want to impose on you, ma'am," McClain replied.

"No bother. We haven't got but four cowhands left, an' they're all out on the range except for Frank here."

"Who's your ramrod?" Jared asked.

"Right now we don't have one. The one we had, Ed Nealy, he ran off when things got tough. He never even said adios," Frank Selby said. "Run like a scared rabbit."

"And it wasn't like Ed to do a thing like that," Fran remarked. "I never could understand it."

Kim Darnell changed the subject. "Why don't we invite them to supper, Momma?"

Mrs. Darnell looked at Jared and McClain.

"Well?"

"I'd be honored," McClain said.

"So would I," Jared answered.

They had a simple evening meal of beef stew, biscuits, apple pie and coffee. After they had eaten and cleaned up the kitchen, Fran, her father and Jared sat on the porch. McClain and Kim walked down towards the corral.

"Let me introduce you to Wildfire," McClain said to the girl.

He took her over to where his dun mustang, Wildfire, was waiting by the water trough. She stood watching as he gave the animal some verbal instructions. The animal stomped its right hoof six times to show its age. It whinnied on command and nudged Kim up against McClain. Finally, Wildfire got down on his front knees so Kim could climb easily into the saddle.

"Oh, he's wonderful," the girl said.

"Take him for a spin, Miss Kim," McClain said.

"Can I, really?"

"Yes, ma'am. He's a real gentleman. He'll go easy on you."

"Alright, then!"

15

Kim Darnell rode slowly out through the gate and down the road. All eyes were on her as she disappeared in the distance.

"She's gone quite a way," Fran said with a look of concern.

"She'll be fine," McClain assured her. "He won't go far from me."

"Here she comes," Jared said.

A quick glance told them that the girl was coming on fast. There were three men in pursuit, trying to overtake her.

McClain whistled loud and Wildfire shot ahead, leaving them in a cloud of red dust. The animal slowed down as it approached the gate. One of the riders came on fast and grabbed the reins of the horse in an attempt to stop it.

"I wouldn't do that," McClain said calmly.

The thin, gangly cowboy glared at McClain. "Who the hell are you talkin' to, mister?"

One of the other cowboys, short and stocky, looked McClain over.

"Looky here! Ol' lady Darnell has hired herself a gunny! Ain't thet a hoot?"

Jared walked slowly down into the yard to look on.

The thin one couldn't resist another remark. "He looks like one of them phony drugstore cowboys from Chicago!"

The third man was older. He looked more intelligent than the others and had an air of authority about him.

McClain looked at Kim and said, "Bring him in, please, Miss Kim."

Kim Darnell walked Wildfire into the yard.

Fran Darnell stood on the porch steps and yelled.

"What do you want, Bill Jorth?"

The older man, identified as Jorth, spoke up. He didn't sound angry or resentful but he spoke with authority.

"Mrs. Darnell, I'm here to complain about your cattle coming over the line to drink at my water holes."

"Those water holes were free until you claimed them, Bill Jorth. They're on open range."

"I filed a claim on that land, ma'am. Now it's mine."

"We'll, if you had any humanity, you'd share it," Fran said.

For a moment Bill Jorth seemed to soften. It quickly passed.

"All I'm saying is I will rebrand any of your cattle that I catch at my water holes. Good-day, ma'am."

The three men started to turn their horses and ride away.

"Hold it!" McClain yelled.

The three stopped and turned back.

"Whatta ya want, asshole?" the tall, slim one smirked. His short friend chuckled.

"I'd like you to apologize to the lady," McClain said.

"What fer?"

"For manhandling her and swearing in her presence," McClain said calmly.

"What if I don't want to, Drugstore?" Slim asked.

"Then I'm calling you out," McClain said simply.

The cowboy chuckled. "What? Yer bracin' me, you fool?"

McClain nodded. "Yes," he said in a calm voice.

"Go ahead and apologize, Mike," Jorth said. "You're no good to me dead."

"No, sir. I won't."

Bill Jorth's hand flew out and he slapped the cowboy across the face. The blow almost knocked the man out of his saddle.

"Goddammit, I said apologize, and do it now!"

The cowboy rocked sideways in the saddle, regained his balance, and then rode off. The rancher turned to Kim Darnell.

"I offer you my apology, ma'am." Jorth looked at McClain. "If I was you, mister, I wouldn't come into town anytime soon." He turned to focus on Jared. "You're pretty quiet, mister. What's your name?"

"Jared. Clay Jared."

"You looking for a job, Jared?"

"I got one. Riding for the Diamond D."

"So am I," McClain said.

Bill Jorth studied them both for a moment, then he and the short cowboy rode away.

3.

"So that's Bill Jorth," Jared said. He was sitting on the porch with Kim, Fran, old Seth and McClain.

"Yes," Fran said, "and the skinny, mean one is Mike Smears, his ramrod. The short one was Ron Medford, Smears' sidekick. Medford doesn't say much but he doesn't miss a thing. And they're both fast on the draw."

"Jorth seems like a civilized fellow, though," Jared said.

"Except when it comes to water," Fran replied sarcastically. "Also, he listens too much to Smears." Fran stopped a moment to reflect on something. "He lost his wife two years back. She got sick. He has no children."

"Maybe that's why he's so bitter," McClain said. "He seems lonely."

Fran's father sniffed the air.

"Yes siree-bob," he said mysteriously. "It smells jest like back in fifty-five. Only then, we had locusts and hoppers by the millions. It was like the Bible comin' ta life."

The old man paused to stare out at a vision from the past.

"They ate everything in sight and what they didn't eat the prairie fires burnt ta cinders. Then came the drought. We didn't see a drop of God's rain for more than forty days and forty nights."

Fran patted the old man's gnarled hand.

"Now, Dad, don't start that again."

"You were only a baby when the devil wind came. It blew so hot across the land everything it touched withered up and died. Dust piled high against the sides of houses and poured down the chimneys. People couldn't even breathe in their own houses. Many died in their beds. Animals, too. Horses, dogs, cows, all died. The sun shined so hot it burnt yer eyeballs if ya opened yer eyes."

Old Seth Darnell wound down with a big sigh. The vison had passed out of sight. He shuddered.

"It was the sinners who caused it all, accordin' to the preachers. Why, those sky pilots wailed and cried like sheep going to the slaughter. Woe! Woe! Woe! Stop yer drinkin'! Stop yer gamblin'! Stop yer fornicatin'!"

He suddenly stopped as quickly as he had begun. Exhausted, he sighed and looked out on the yard. Fran stroked his hand again.

Evening was settling in. Bats started to fly out of the barn and circle it like black kites in a whirlwind.

"They live in the rafters," Fran said.

There was a soft, orange glow in the west, just above the pines at the edge of the field.

"I'll go into Salisbury tomorrow, Dad," Fran said, "see if Mr. Carter at the bank will give us a little breathing room."

"What's that all about, if I might ask, ma'am?" Jared said.

"Mr. Carter runs the Cattlemen's Saving and Loan Bank in town. He holds our mortgage. Since there won't be a cattle drive to Ellsworth this year, I'm afraid I'll be behind in payments."

"Sorry to hear that, ma'am," Jared said.

"I'll go into town with ya, Momma," Kim said. "I'll mosey around Dobson's Mercantile a while. See what's new."

Fran nodded. "Sure, baby."

She turned to Jared and McClain. "That offer to use the bunkhouse is still open to both of you."

"Thank you, ma'am," McClain replied. "I'll just take you up on that."

"An' feel free to use the corral and barn. There's oats in there for your horses."

It was time to say goodnight.

Jared and McClain walked their horses down to the barn, unsaddled and fed them. Before they left for the bunkhouse, they brushed the animals down and put them in the corral.

Frank Selby watched as they came in, and stowed their saddles and gear under two of the many empty cots. He came over, sat next to them and started rolling a cigarette.

"What's the situation, Selby?" Jared asked.

Selby lit his cigarette and blew out a cloud of smoke.

"Well, the situation is she ain't got no ramrod, all her cowhands are gone, and she's behind on payments to the bank. That's about it."

"Why are you still here?" Jared asked.

Selby thought about that for a moment.

"I don't know." He shrugged.

"It looks like she's between a rock and a hard place," McClain said.

Selby nodded. "Yeah. I reckon she knows she's done fer."

"So, what about you, Selby?" Jared asked again. "You gonna cut out?"

"I'm thinkin' on it. But I'd hate to leave her swingin' in the wind. Maybe I'll hang on for a while. See what happens."

"They do much gambling in town?" McClain asked.

Selby chuckled. "Hell, yes, on Friday nights at the Sagebrush Saloon. Especially at the end of the month."

"That's tomorrow," McLain said.

"Yeah, that's right. Why?"

"Oh, nothing," McClain replied.

He reached into his saddlebag and took out a pack of cards. Jared and Selby watched him remove the deck and do some fancy shuffling.

"Jesus," Selby said. "Remind me not to play cards against you, friend."

"Would you play cards with me?"

"Whatta ya mean, 'with you'?" Selby asked.

"I'm going to town tomorrow night and get up a little game of five-card draw," McClain replied. "I'd like you and Jared to sit in. You'll bring your winnings back here and we'll give it to Mrs. Darnell."

"What makes you think we'll win?" Jared chuckled.

"Don't worry about that. Just sit in and play. I'll do the rest."

Selby was suddenly cautious. "I don't know. It's sounds fishy, takin' cowpokes for their money."

"They'll piss it away on rotgut, cards and women anyway," McClain said. "It wouldn't hurt to give Mrs. Darnell a chunk, would it?"

Selby shrugged and looked at Jared. "What about you, Jared? You in?" He was hoping Jared would refuse.

Jared nodded. "I'll do it, but just this once."

For a moment, Selby looked cornered.

"Well, Selby? You in or out?" McClain asked again.

"I don't know."

"You won't do it for the brand? For her?"

"I don't think so. It sounds too risky," Selby said with conviction. "No. Sorry, pal."

McClain forced a smile. "Okay, sure. It's your call, Selby."

"That's right, it's my call," Selby responded. He didn't sound very friendly.

McClain just chuckled and put the cards away.

4.

It was mid-morning and already hot when Fran Darnell and her daughter Kim rode their buckboard out of the yard, heading for Dobson's Mercantile in Salisbury. The wheels of the small wagon churned up a trail of red dust that hung in the air. Above them, the sky was as bright and empty as it had been for the last two months.

They could hear the shrill sound of the cicadas in the black walnut trees in the fields alongside the road. The heat had brought them to life.

They reached the old Ellsworth coach road five miles north of the Diamond D. It stretched east to where it cut past the outskirts of Salisbury and went on to Caldwell to the south.

It was only a half hour's ride into town.

Salisbury had once been an important stagecoach way station years ago. Gold was found nearby and people came by the hundreds. The town grew but the gold ran out. Then the farmers and ranchers came to fill the void.

Now it had a saloon, Chinese laundry, barbershop, bathhouse, surveyor's office, real estate office, train depot, bank, jail and a church. It was pretty much like every other town where a railroad spur came in off the main trunk to ship cattle and produce to eastern markets.

Basically, it now served the local ranchers and farmers, who kept the place alive and thriving. The railroad spur from Ellsworth, sixty miles north, made it easy to get in and out of the area.

The women were a few miles west of town when two riders came out from behind a rise to block the road. Fran Darnell pulled the buckboard to a sudden stop.

The two intruders were scraggly and filthy, and their faces were hidden behind beards. One wore a soiled Union Army jacket and hat and carried a pistol. The other, a bigger, heavier man dressed in rags, pointed a rifle.

"Hello, ladies," the big one croaked like a frog. His yellow, rotted teeth showed when he spoke. "Where ya headed?"

"Get out of our way!" Fran demanded.

The big one chuckled.

The thin one in the Union jacket and hat leaned over and grabbed the buckboard harness, holding it tight. He stared at Kim, licked his crusted, split, dry lips and smiled.

"How's about a little friendliness, ma'am?" the big one said.

"Get away from us, you stinking sidewinders!" Kim yelled.

The big one snickered. "Wal, now, thet ain't no way fer a lady ta talk, is it?"

Fran tried to back the buckboard up but couldn't. The thin one had a firm grip on the harness. She thought about grabbing the rifle she had stashed in the boot well but couldn't get to it. Anyway, they had her covered.

"Let go!" she screamed.

The thin one chuckled and backed his horse off the road into an opening in the pine trees. He pulled the horse and buckboard along with him. Fran fought for control but couldn't get it.

The big one called over to his partner. "Someone is coming, Cal!"

They all turned to look at a lone rider coming from the west, behind them.

"Hell, Tom," Cal said. "It's only jest one. Probably some dumb cowboy."

Kim saw who it was. "I'd run like hell if I was you, mister!"

The big man turned to face the oncoming rider. He raised his rifle, squinted down the road and fired off a shot.

"Ya missed, Cal! Try agin'!"

Suddenly a bullet, followed by the bark of a gun, smacked the big man in the chest with a sickening thud. He flipped backwards over his horse, hit the road on his head, and fell in a twisted heap.

The thin one let go of the buckboard harness, turned his horse and rode into the woods.

A moment later McClain came riding up. He nodded to the women as he rode by and disappeared into the pine trees. A few minutes later they heard a second gunshot. After that, McClain returned with the outlaw's horse in tow.

"Good afternoon, ladies," he said calmly.

"Good afternoon, Mr. McClain," Fran replied.

"Are you ladies alright?"

"We are now, thank you," Fran said.

"Good. Then I'll just escort you to town, if I may?"

"You may, indeed, Mr. McClain," Fran answered.

McClain tied both of the outlaws' horses to the back of the buckboard. Fran got the rig back on the road and they headed for town at a slow pace. In twenty minutes they tied up at the Cattlemen's Saving and Loan building.

"Thank you, Mr. McClain," Fran said. "I'm grateful for your help."

Both women got down from the buckboard.

"I'm going over to Dobson's Mercantile, Momma," Kim said.

"Alright, I'll meet you there," Fran replied.

As both women walked away, McClain untied the horses from the back of the buckboard. He swung up into his saddle, grabbed the reins of the outlaws' horses and led them down the road to the jailhouse. Once there he dismounted, tied all three horses to the rail, glanced at the sign above the door and went in.

"Marshal Landry," McClain said, "I just left two dead men about five miles west of town. They were attacking the Darnell women."

"Was one of them wearin' a Union coat?"

"That's right."

The old, silver-haired marshal chuckled.

"Thank God! Them was the two that was hangin' around in the woods robbin' folks. Nice job. I'll send my deputy out there with a buckboard ta tote 'em in." He looked McClain over. "You a bounty hunter?"

"No," McClain said. "Why?"

"The town had a bounty on both them critters."

"Oh? How much?"

"Five hundred each."

McClain whistled. "That's a lot. What did they do?"

"Fer one, they raped the mayor's daughter," Marshal Landry said. "Fer another, they been bustin' in people's houses and businesses at night when the town was asleep. They were as slippery as two eels."

"I've got their horses and gear tied out front."

"Good. They'll sell fer jest about enough ta pay fer the buryin'," the marshal said.

McClain nodded. "Sure. Ah, when do I get that bounty?"

"As soon as I see the bodies an' you make out a statement. Ya got any witnesses?"

"Yes. Mrs. Darnell and her daughter," McClain said. "About that statement, I'll do it now but the money goes to Mrs. Darnell, not me."

It took McClain twenty minutes to complete the statement. He signed it and handed it to the marshal.

"When will they get the money?"

"Tomorrow. It'll be waitin' at the bank."

McClain shook hands with the lawman then left. Outside he mounted his horse and walked it up the street to the Sagebrush Saloon.

After looking around for a moment, McClain slid down, tied up and went in through the batwing doors. He stood inside for a moment letting his eyes adjust to the gloom. The place smelled of stale tobacco juice and whiskey but was a bit cooler than the street, which was, by now, blistering hot. All the tables were empty except one where four townsfolk in suits sat drinking and talking. Two cowboys stood at the bar doing the same.

McClain bellied up, dropped an eagle on the bar and ordered a local beer. He grabbed a jerky stick from a jar close by and munched away as he drank.

"Yer new," the bartender said. He was small and thin, had a boyish face, slicked-back brown hair and wore glasses. He looked more like a bank clerk than anything else.

"Virgil McClain. I'm out at the Diamond D." McClain looked around. "Kind of quiet, isn't it?"

"I'm Earl Perry. Come back tonight," Perry said. "They'll come in here with a month's wages. So will the girls and the cardsharps. Most of them will leave broke but happy."

"Who settles the disputes, Earl?"

"Bessy O'Toole."

McClain chuckled. "Who the hell is Bessy O'Toole?"

Perry reached under the bar and brought up a double-barreled scattergun. "Say hello to Bessy O'Toole, friend."

McClain nodded and Perry but the gun back under the bar.

Suddenly one of the two cowboys at the bar turned and took notice of McClain. It was the cowboy who was with Bill Jorth and his ramrod, Mike Smears, the one named Ron Medford.

"Well, well, if it ain't the Drugstore Kid!" Medford said with a sneer. "An' all alone, too."

McClain pretended not to hear. He stared ahead into the mirror behind the bar and took a drink of beer.

Medford looked at the bartender. "Hey, Earl, this is the same asshole who wanted Mike Smears ta apologize fer roughin' up the little Darnell bitch. Kin you believe thet?"

The bartender looked at McClain, waiting for him to respond. He didn't.

Medford walked up to him and said, "Hey, asshole! I'm a-talkin' to you."

Young Earl Perry suddenly looked nervous.

"Come on now, Ron. Be civil," he said. "You can see the man doesn't want any trouble. He's just having a peaceful drink. He's not bothering anybody."

Ron Medford sneered.

"Well, he's a-botherin' the hell outta me. He ain't so tough when he's alone. He thinks he's a big man. Well, he ain't shit in my book. He's lucky Mike Smears didn't drill his ass. An' he woulda if old man Jorth had a-minded his own business."

Medford's companion put a hand on his arm. "Take it easy, Ron."

"I told ya about him, Tom. How he wanted Smears ta apologize ta thet sweet, little Darnell bitch."

Tom looked scared. "Maybe we'd best be gettin' back to the Circle J, Ron," he said urgently.

Medford ignored his friend's advice. "If Mike was here he'd brace ya, ya sonofabitch!"

McClain turned slowly to face the cowboy. "Well, seeing as you're here, why don't you brace me?"

For a moment Medford was surprised, but he quickly recovered.

"Okay! Draw, you stinkin' sidewinder!" Medford yelled.

Ron Medford went for his gun but it wasn't there. It had somehow jumped into McClain's hand and then slammed against the side of his head. Medford's eyes rolled up in his head as his knees buckled and he sank unconsciously to the floor.

McClain emptied Medford's gun on the bar.

"Take him home," McClain said. He handed the gun to Medford's friend and together they carried Medford outside and laid him across his saddle.

McClain watched for a moment as they rode away, then untied his horse and led it down to Dobson's Mercantile. He stood by the porch rolling a cigarette as he waited. Soon Mrs. Darnell came walking down from the Cattlemen's Savings and Loan. She didn't look very happy.

"Bad news?" McClain asked.

"I don't blame Mr. Carter. I guess I'm a poor risk," Fran said.

"What will happen?"

"I've got thirty days to catch up on back payments. If I don't, the bank takes it all."

"I see."

Kim walked out of the mercantile and they all left for the Diamond D.

The afternoon sun was bearing down on the town. It got a bit cooler five miles west, except that the wind blew the dry, hot dust in their faces as they rode along. McClain rode alongside the women. When they arrived at the place where the outlaws were shot, they met the marshal and his deputy loading the bodies on a buckboard. The lawman waved them down.

"Come into town tomorrow, Mrs. Darnell," the marshal said. "I'll have yer thousand dollars waitin' fer ya, ma'am."

"My thousand dollars? I don't understand, Marshal."

"Talk ta Mr. McClain about thet, ma'am," Marshal Landry said.

Fran looked at McClain.

"It's a long story, ma'am," McClain said. "I'll tell you on the way back to the ranch."

As he told them about the reward, young Kim Darnell stared adoringly at Virgil McClain. She knew she was in love with her brave knight in shining armor.

Later that night she would lie in bed reliving the moments when McClain came riding to her rescue on his trusty steed, Wildfire, on a dusty road outside the kingdom of Camelot, also known as the Diamond D Ranch.

5.

About seven that evening, McClain and Jared elbowed their way into the Sagebrush Saloon. The smoke was thick enough to slice with a knife and the noise loud enough to be heard in Kansas City. It was packed so full that cowboys and townsfolk spilled out onto the porch and into the street.

It took a while to get Earl Perry's attention but they finally got a bottle of whiskey and two glasses.

They left the bar and pushed their way through the crowd until they found a table by the wall that someone had left empty. An oil lamp above gave just enough light to play cards by. They quickly plopped down in two of the five chairs, facing each other.

"This is perfect," McClain said.

He poured them a drink and they both put some coins on the table. McClain took a deck of cards from his vest pocket and dealt Jared and himself five cards. They played Deuces Wild, pretending to wager. To anyone glancing over, it looked like a real game was going on.

"There's something fishy about Frank Selby," Jared said as they played.

"Oh? How so?"

"It's just a feeling I have about him," Jared replied. "Just a wild hunch."

Two cowboys came over and watched for a while. Once they saw it was Deuces Wild with low stakes, they asked whose game it was.

"Mine," McClain said.

"Can we sit in?"

"Sure."

The two sat in. In a few minutes one more came, making the table a full five.

The game had no more than started when Mike Smears and Ron Medford walked up to the table. The side of Medford's head was black and blue. He looked mad.

"Well, if it ain't fancy pants and his sidekick," Smears chuckled sarcastically.

"What do you want, Smears?" McClain said calmly as he put his cards face down.

"You were warned not ta come ta town, weren't ya, fancy pants?"

The three cowboys suddenly tossed in their hands, grabbed up their money and then scattered. Tables nearby cleared out. They saw the signs of a gunfight. It was what Mike Smears had a reputation for.

Jared and McClain picked up their money, too. McClain gathered the cards up, put them back in the deck and put the deck in his vest pocket.

McClain looked up at Smears.

"Mrs. Darnell is still waiting for your apology, Smears," he said.

Smears sneered and spit on the floor near McClain's boot.

"Hell, I ain't gonna apologize ta thet bitch as long as I'm alive, asshole."

"That might not be long," McClain replied.

He stood up. In a second, Jared was up beside him, facing Smears and Medford.

"Who asked you ta butt in, Jared?" Medford asked.

"We're pards," Jared said.

"Then yer gonna die with him," Smears growled.

Earl Perry came over from the bar and stood between them.

"Best take it out on the street," he said.

Smears chuckled and patted the bartender on the shoulder.

"Sure, Earl. We don't wanna shoot up the place, do we, Ron?"

Medford nodded. "Hell no, Mike. We'll jest take this dance out front fer the ladies ta see."

Smears smirked confidently at Jared and McClain.

"And Earl, ya best send somebody over ta tell the box maker ta make two. He'll be needin' them real soon." Smears turned and walked towards the batwings. "Let's git it done."

The others followed.

Jared stood in the street alongside McClain wondering what the hell he was doing there. He looked up at the sky. The sun was low in the west. Evening was near. A dog barked in a nearby alley. Cowboys and painted ladies stood on the saloon porch, anxiously waiting for the killing to start.

"I wonder if they're taking bets." McClain chuckled.

Jared turned his back for a moment to adjust his holster.

"You can bet they are," Jared said. He turned around again. "Do you mind if I take big mouth?"

"Smears? No. He's mine."

"Then you better stick it to him quick. If he draws as fast as he talks, then you're in real trouble, friend."

McClain chuckled. "Maybe I should shoot him in the mouth, then."

"That's a good idea," Jared replied.

They watched Smears and Medford get in position about thirty feet down the road. For a moment they got on the wrong side and had to switch around so that Smears was facing McClain. A few people on the porch laughed.

Finally, the four men stood staring at each other with quiet intensity.

"Go ahead and say it again, Smears," McClain hollered.

Smears yelled back, "Fran Darnell is a whore an' her daughter is a bitch!"

All four men drew at once.

Smears fanned off a quick shot at McClain. The bullet missed his head but took his hat clean off. Before he could get another shot off, McClain fired back, hitting him in the left leg, shattering the bone. As Smears grunted and toppled sideways, McClain shot him in the chest, near the heart. The Circle J ramrod fired his gun into the ground and went down on his back in the road. After that he didn't move.

Medford was a lot slower than Jared was. Jared hesitated, and then fanned off a shot, purposely hitting Medford in his right arm. The impact sent him groaning to his knees. He dropped his gun and held up his hand for mercy.

"I'm done, Jared!" Medford groaned. "Help me out, won't ya?"

Jared holstered his Colt and walked towards the wounded man, intending to assist him. When he was about ten feet away, Medford pulled a derringer from his boot and pointed it at Jared's face.

A gun barked. Jared felt the heat and wind of McClain's bullet as it sped by and hit Medford in the heart. Medford dropped the derringer and fell on his back in the road.

As Medford lay there, he raised one hand. Jared knelt down beside him. Medford whispered something. Jared bent closer to hear. He nodded. In a few seconds, Medford was dead.

"Alright, boys!" Marshal Landry was upon them. "I'll take yer guns."

"What for, Marshal?" It was the bartender, Earl Perry, defending the winners. "Smears and Medford braced McClain and Jared. Simple as that. Ask anybody here."

"That's right, Marshal, we saw it all," a cowboy who had been in the card game said.

The marshal gave this consideration, then nodded.

"Is there any Circle J cowboys here?" the marshal shouted at the crowd.

Four men came off the porch. The marshal pointed at the bodies.

"Take 'em home, boys. Tell Mr. Jorth what happened," the old marshal said. "I'll see him tomorrow."

After the Circle J cowhands had taken the bodies away, the marshal looked at Jared and McClain. "You two come over to the jailhouse. I'll be needin' yer statements. I'll get yours later, Earl. An' you, too, cowboy."

McClain and Jared followed the marshal down to the jailhouse and wrote out their versions of what had happened.

"You two don't know what you jest started," the marshal said. "Jorth ain't gonna let it stand. Not by a long shot."

"We didn't start this, Marshal," Jared said. "We already proved that."

"I know but it won't make no difference ta Jorth. You just brought Fran Darnell a mountain of trouble. I hope ya know that. The best thing for you two is ta ride on as fast as ya kin."

Instead of running, Jared and McClain went back to the Sagebrush Saloon to play cards.

By four in the morning they had racked up a little over seven hundred dollars. It had been a long night.

They headed back to the Diamond D.

6.

"You got careless back there, Jared," McClain said as they rode back towards the ranch. "It almost got you killed."

"Yeah. You're right."

The road west looked like a silver ribbon in the moonlight. Coyotes howled in the nearby hills. A deer came out of the brush down the road, and when it saw them, it sprinted away into the night. The air was heavy as the earth tried to shake off the heat of the day.

"The next time put two slugs in him."

Jared nodded. He didn't like being preached to so he kept quiet. But McClain wasn't finished yet.

"Now that Smears and Medford are out of the way, it's the old man's turn," McClain said.

"Who? Jorth?"

"Yeah."

"Why Jorth?"

"You heard what Mrs. Darnell said. She thinks Jorth killed her husband or had Smears do it."

"If she's right, it's best to get solid evidence on Jorth and let the law deal with him."

"I don't see how we can, unless he admits to it."

"Yeah. That's the thing."

McClain chuckled.

"What's so funny?" Jared asked.

"Us. Why the hell are we sticking our noses into somebody else's mess? All we have to do is split the money we won tonight and ride away."

"So why don't you ride out?" Jared asked. McClain shrugged. "It's the girl, Kim, isn't it?"

McClain was just about to answer when a bullet whipped by their heads and a gunshot rang out in the night.

McClain yelled. "Move it!"

They kicked their horses into a gallop down the road, spreading out as far as they could. They heard four more shots. McClain grunted.

"You hit?" Jared shouted.

"Yeah!"

"Bad?"

"Maybe. I don't know. Let's get into the trees!"

Jared turned his mount to the right, heading into the shadows of a pine stand. Twenty feet in they stopped and waited, watching the road. McClain leaned over his saddle and held his right side.

"Shit!" McClain said. "I'm bleeding bad. Tie me in."

Jared got the spare manila lariat out of his saddlebag, the one he used for light work, and cut off a long piece. He tied McClain's hands to the saddle horn and his feet into the stirrups, running the rope under the horse's barrel.

With that done, he grabbed the reins of McClain's horse and, mounting his own, started out onto the road at a fast trot.

It was sunup by the time they rode into the yard of the Diamond D. McClain was slumped sideways in his saddle. Jared quickly slipped the knots of the rope and lowered him to the ground. McClain leaned on his horse for support.

"Can you walk? I'll help."

"Thanks."

Jared took McClain's left arm, placed it around his neck and helped him across the yard and up the porch steps. They were met in the hallway by Fran Darnell.

"What happened?"

"We were ambushed on the way back from town," Jared said. McClain smiled weakly. He looked pale.

"Bring him in the kitchen," Fran said and ran ahead of them.

Jared lowered McClain into a chair at the table as Fran got the medicine box from the cupboard. Kim came down from upstairs looking sleepy. When she saw McClain, she ran to him.

"I'm fine, Miss Kim," McClain said.

"Move out of the way," Fran said to Kim. "Get his shirt off!"

Jared unbuttoned McClain's shirt and draped it over a chair. Fran started to work on his wound. She sloshed an antiseptic solution on a gauze pad and swabbed it down good. McClain grunted from the burning sensation.

"You're in luck, Mr. McClain. The bullet went clean through. But it's pretty bad."

McClain smiled but didn't say anything.

"It ain't bleeding all that much now," Fran said as she wrapped a bandage around McClain's waist. "But maybe you should see Doc Samples in town."

"We'll see," McClain said.

Kim felt McClain's forehead. "He's got a fever, Momma." She held McClain's hand. "We should put him in an upstairs bedroom."

Fran saw what was happening. So did McClain and Jared.

"I don't want to be a bother, ma'am," McClain said.

"It'll be no bother, Mr. McClain," Fran replied. She smiled. "Now we've got two wounded cowboys, Mr. Selby and Mr. McClain."

"Yes," Jared said, wondering where Frank Selby was. "Is Selby here?"

"He most likely spent the night in town." Fran replied. "Friday nights get wild in Salisbury."

"Sure," Jared said.

Old Seth Darnell rolled his wheelchair into the kitchen.

"What's all the ruckus about?" he asked.

"Mr. McClain was ambushed an' shot," Kim said.

"Ambushed and shot by who?"

"We don't know, Dad," Fran replied.

"Well it smells like Jorth's work ta me! I don't trust thet sidewinder!"

The old man's eyes bulged with emotion. He began to shake. The wheelchair groaned under the strain.

"We don't know that for sure, dad."

"Oh, it'll all come out when the devil wind starts ta blow. Mark me, it'll blow soon, and when it blows, all the evil in the world will come up from the pits of hell. When that happens there'll be a bloodbath the likes of which mankind has never seen before!"

Fran patted her father's hand. "Now calm down, Dad."

Her touch had a soothing effect. The old man sighed and smiled weakly.

Jared and Kim helped McClain upstairs to a small bedroom. She stayed with him as Jared went back downstairs to the kitchen. Old Seth Darnell was out on the porch.

Fran made breakfast while Jared drank his coffee.

"Mr. Jared," Fran said. "I haven't been very honest with you. There's something I should tell you."

"Alright, ma'am. Go ahead."

"First, I don't have any cowhands out on the range. They've moved on. I haven't paid them in three months. Second, I can't hire you or Mr. McClain because I got no money. Third, my cattle are all gone, dead for want of water or scattered by Bill Jorth's men. Fourth, the bank is gonna take the Diamond D."

"Is that all? I thought it was something serious," Jared chuckled.

"Yep, that's about it," Fran said, smiling. "It is kind of funny, isn't it? Funny enough to cry about."

"Well, don't cry just yet, Mrs. Darnell," Jared said.

He took a roll of bills out of his vest, the one he had slipped out of McClain's shirt pocket when he had helped him take it off. He laid the money on the table. Fran stared at it.

"What's that, Mr. Jared?"

"That's almost eight-hundred dollars we won for you last night at poker, ma'am. And there's another thousand waiting for you in town, the reward McClain told you about for killing those two outlaws. Now you can hold the bank off for a while."

For a moment Fran looked about to cry. She choked back her tears and cleared her throat.

"Why, Mr. Jared? Why? You don't owe me anything. And you surely don't know me. So, why?"

"I don't know why, ma'am," Jared said. "I really don't. It's just a feeling, an attitude. It's how I am. It's my code."

"Some men have a different code, Mr. Jared. Men like Jorth."

"You think so, ma'am."

"Yes I do."

Jared avoided her eyes for a moment, Then, to change the subject, he asked, "Do you have a place to keep this?"

"There's a small safe in my husband's study. I'll put it in there."

Fran took the money and left. Ten minutes later she returned and finished making breakfast.

After they had finished the ham, eggs, grits and coffee, Kim took a plate up to McClain's room. Old Seth went into the great room to read the Bible. Jared and Fran sat at the kitchen table talking again.

"So you think all your cattle are either scattered, stolen or dead?"

"Yes."

"And you don't have one water hole out there someplace?"

"No. Not one."

"How do you know?"

"Because Frank Selby said so. He's the ramrod of the Diamond D now since Ed Nealy left. Selby says he's rode every square inch of the spread and found nothing."

"Didn't you mention that Nealy sort of disappeared?"

"Yes. Mr. Selby said Nealy told him he was riding east, away from the drought, to find work."

They heard someone ride into the yard.

"That's probably Mr. Selby," Fran said.

She suddenly stood up.

"His arm. It must be pretty bad to have to wear a sling all the time," Jared said.

"I guess. I really don't know. He said he had Doc Samples look at it in town," Fran replied. "Mr. Selby is a good man. He's been a big help during these tough times."

Jared got up from the table.

"Ma'am, I should go look after McClain's horse. And mine, too."

"Thank you for everything, Mr. Jared. I'm deeply in your debt."

"Thanks, ma'am, but it was really all McClain's doing."

For a moment they looked at each other. Jared wanted to reach out and hold her, and tell her everything would be all right. But he felt he didn't have the right to do that. Instead, he left and took the horses down to the barn to feed and water them. After stripping the gear and brushing them down, he left them in the corral and walked up to the bunkhouse.

As he went in, he noticed Selby's horse tied to the rail out front. Inside he saw that the door to the ramrod's room was open. He looked in and saw Selby sprawled out on a cot. He was asleep and snoring loudly.

Jared went back outside and took Selby's horse down to the barn to tend to it. As he was stripping the gear off he caught the lingering scent of gunpowder. He pulled the rifle from its sheath.

The barrel felt slightly warmer than it should normally be. He opened the breach and put it close to his face then shoved a finger into the receiver. It came out with gunpowder residue on it. Selby had probably fired his rifle within the past few hours, early in the morning at the latest.

After putting Selby's horse in the corral, Jared went back to the bunkhouse to lay down. It had been a long night.

Before he fell asleep he thought about what Medford had whispered in his ear before he died. At the right moment he would tell Fran Darnell. But not yet.

7.

The next morning after breakfast Fran Darnell took Jared aside. She was dressed in men's clothing and had a well-packed saddlebag slung over her shoulder.

"Mr. Jared," she said, "I'm going for a ride. Will you come with me?"

"Sure, ma'am." Jared replied.

Jared studied her for a moment. She was all of five years older than he was but anyone could see she was of good, sturdy, western stock. Her hair was tied into a ponytail and she wore a wide-brimmed hat. The man's vest, shirt, pants and boots fitted her well. The flush of her skin and the sparkle in her eyes said that she had spent time in the outdoors and loved it.

Fran also wore a belted Colt .45 revolver.

Jared got his horse and another quarter horse for Fran from the corral. They took the animals into the barn to water, feed and saddle them up. Fran insisted they also take along bedrolls and double canteens.

They rode out of the Diamond D yard around mid-morning.

"Where you taking me, ma'am?" Jared asked. This was all very mysterious.

"I'm not sure yet."

"Well, that's nice," Jared said with a chuckle.

They rode northwest across a vast field of dead bromegrass and sage. A magnificent cottonwood tree stood towering in the middle, its leafless branches a testament to the drought. There were no sheltering clouds in the sky and the two riders began to feel the downward pressure of the stifling heat. The land was cracked open and sucked dry by the hot devil winds of old Seth Darnell's past.

They began to see vultures flying high overhead. In a while they saw them on the ground feeding on dead cows. Skeletons dotted the landscape. As they rode along, the riders saw more and more.

After two hours, they came to the west line shack. The horses were exhausted. Fran and the cowboy dismounted. Jared poured a canteen of water in his hat and let the animals drink.

As they approached the line shack door they heard the sound of tiny scurrying feet. Jared flung the door open and they saw a horde of huge rats running back and forth, leaving their footprints on the dust-covered floor, table and chairs.

The rodents paid no attention to the intruders but went about their business of eating. They had chewed a hole through the back wall and gotten into the larder.

A bag of cornmeal seemed to be alive. It shook and quivered as the animals moved about within it. A slab of smoked pork was completely covered in rats. It danced about on its tether as rodents leaped upon it from the shelf of the larder, knocking other rats off onto the floor. The sharp-toothed things had even eaten through the metal cans of peaches and sweet potatoes.

Rodent feces lay all over the floor, chairs and table.

"Let's go," Fran said, holding a hand over her mouth to shut out the stench.

They mounted up and rode down to the stream behind the line shack. As expected, it was bone-dry. They rode on.

"I had to see this for myself," Fran said. "To see how bad it was."

Jared looked over at her. She turned her head, avoiding his eyes.

As they rode on, things got worse. They came upon thousands of dead cows and almost as many vultures. Some animals were eaten completely clean and their bleached bones lay pointing at the sky above.

The big, black, redheaded vultures boldly ignored the riders. Sometimes they dropped down close to them, bobbing their long necks and watching with curiosity, hopping along behind them, never making a sound.

Sometimes they saw coyotes feasting on the carcasses as the buzzards patiently waited their turn.

The north line shack was in much better shape than the west one. The larder was empty but there were no rats, only an inch-thick carpet of dust covering everything inside. After giving it a quick look, they went out and gave the horses some more water.

"Did you notice something different here?" Jared asked Fran.

"No. What is it?"

"There weren't many dead cows for the last two miles or so. Maybe a dozen or more."

"Maybe they drifted down country looking for water," Fran replied. "That's where they probably died, with the others."

"That could be."

They rode down behind the line shack to check the stream there. It was dry, just like all the others. Jared took the lead and rode into a stand of birch trees. Their dead leaves lay like a carpet on the dry ground, their branches bare.

A large, open area lay behind the trees. Beyond that, a rock wall rose up about twenty feet high. It stretched east and west for miles.

"What's back there, behind the rocks?" Jared asked.

"I have no idea. This is the end of the Diamond D."

"Let's take a look."

"It's getting late. You think we should?"

"Maybe there's a cool place with some shade in there. We could camp outside for the night. It's a hundred in the line shack."

"Yes, you're right," Fran replied.

As they rode along, Jared glanced down. Suddenly he stopped.

"What's wrong?"

Jared pointed at the dry earth.

"There's a trail here. You can just barely make it out. Can you see it?"

Fran also looked down. "I think so. Yes. It could be a trail."

"And there are some cattle tracks, too."

"Are you sure, Mr. Jared?"

Jared didn't answer but rode ahead and stopped again.

"There's lots of cattle tracks, ma'am. Horses, too."

They followed the tracks up towards the rock wall to where they turned east. A half mile more and they saw an opening in the wall. It was where the tracks went through.

Both riders were excited now. Urging their mounts on, they rode through the twenty-foot-wide riff in the rock wall. It slanted downward into shadows. The air felt cooler here. A hundred yards more and it was blocked by a fence fashioned from dry birch branches. It had a crude gate.

Jared dismounted and swung it open. Fran rode in, towing his horse. He closed it behind her and mounted up again.

The land inside the opening was rocky and dry but further down they saw green grass and bushes. Further on they saw healthy-looking pines and aspens and yet further below was a small lake surrounded by a green field. But what caused their hearts to beat faster was the small herd of cattle, about nine hundred or more, feeding on the tall, lush grass around the lake.

"Oh, my God!" Fran Darnell cried.

They rode down to the lake and into the herd.

"They've got the Diamond D brand on 'em!" Fran yelled. She started to laugh nervously, not believing what her eyes saw. The horses made their way to the lake and drank. Fran and Jared dismounted and drank with them. The water was cold and sweet.

Jared stood up and looked around.

"Over there!" He said, pointing.

There was a lean-to with canvas over the top. It had been built back under a rock overhang. They walked over to it. A body lay sprawled near a small fire pit. It was badly deteriorated but its clothing was still intact.

"Oh, God!" Jan cried. "That's Ed Nealy!"

"Are you sure?"

"Yes. It's Ed. I can tell by his clothing."

"Then I guess he didn't run off like Selby said."

They walked closer to the body. It was badly decomposed. It lay on its face on the rock floor.

"Someone shot him," Fran said pointing to a hole in Nealy's vest.

"Yeah," Jared replied. He saw a spade nearby.

There was a bedroll under the lean-to. Jared spread it out next to the body. He used the spade to roll the body over, first the torso, then the legs. It took a while but he finally had it wrapped up. He tied it with a piece of manila rope cut from his extra lariat.

"He's pretty ripe," Jared said. "I'll drag him off a way so we don't smell him."

While Jared was gone, Fran got the saddlebag from her horse and unpacked the small coffeepot and coffee. She walked down to the lake and filled it. There was a pile of wood under the overhang. She started a small fire and put the pot on to boil. By the time Jared got back, the coffee was ready. They sat down and ate beef jerky and biscuits.

"I wonder who killed old Ed." Fran thought out loud.

Jared nodded. "Yeah. Good question, ma'am. Another good question is who drove the cattle in here?"

"Do you think it was one of my men?"

"Yeah, but which one?" Jared mused. "That's another question."

Fran smiled and chuckled. She seemed suddenly happy.

"Are you alright, ma'am?" Jared asked.

"Alright? I'm better than all right, Mr. Jared. I feel great. I have my cows right here with me. Those heifers and alpha steers, they're the beginning of a new herd."

"That's right," Jared admitted. "All you have to do is leave them here until the drought is over. When the grass comes back you can move them onto your spread."

Fran grabbed Jared's hand and shook it vigorously.

"Thank you, Mr. Jared, for finding my herd. I would never have found them in a hundred years."

"It was pure luck, ma'am, pure dumb luck," Jared replied. He thought for a moment. "Now all we have to do is find out who murdered Mr. Nealy."

It started to get dark. Jared cut some young pine branches for them to lay their blankets on. He laid out the blankets and went looking for more dead branches for a fire. In an hour he had gathered enough to last the night. They finally lay down, looking up at the night sky. The moon hung low over the lake. It was full and bright.

They talked well into the night.

8.

The devil wind began to blow into the Salisbury area the morning after Fran Darnell and Clay Jared rode off for the north line shack. Its reach was wide and its wrath was terrible. It descended upon the already wounded earth like the hammers of hell.

Old Seth Darnell looked worried.

"Hold on ta yer hats," the crusty only man chuckled. "We're in fer a good ass-kickin'."

Kim Darnell, old Seth and Frank Selby were sitting in the kitchen when the first signs of a blow came across the yard. McClain lay upstairs in his bed asleep. Outside, the windmill blades spun like crazy, whining in the wind. The horses in the corral whinnied and stomped.

"I hope Momma and Jared are okay," Kim said as a blast of hot wind and dust hit the side of the house.

"Best lock the horses in the barn." Her grandfather looked worried. "If they break loose in the storm they'll run hell bent for leather clear across the county."

"Alright," Kim replied.

"I'll go, too," Selby said. He stood up and adjusted his arm sling.

"Are you sure, Mr. Selby?" the young girl asked. "You might hurt yer arm."

"I'm fine."

"Alright."

They hurried out into the yard and over to the corral. A blast of air hit them hard. It felt like tiny needles against their skin. Their eyes automatically went into a squint against it.

Kim heard the horses crying. They sensed what was coming.

There were nine horses in the corral. One by one, they led them out of the enclosure into the barn. It was slow work. One was spooked so badly from the whining of the wind it broke into a run across the yard and beyond.

Kim got some rope and tied the rear barn door shut. She and Selby stood at the front doors staring out at the raging sandstorm. The bunkhouse across the way was hard to see. Sometimes it showed up and then disappeared behind a wall of red dust. Clusters of sage and pine branches rolled across the field and piled up against the yard fence.

Kim looked up for a moment, fascinated. The bats were clinging to the rafters, swaying in the wind, wrapped in their wings. Sometimes one lost its hold and flew in circles before it found a place to land.

"Maybe we should wait here for a while," Selby said. "It might blow over quick." His voice sounded strange.

He suddenly came up close behind Kim. She felt his breath on the back of her neck. He put a hand on her shoulder.

"No." She moved away. "Let's go."

He grabbed her by the shoulders and tried to spin her around. This shocked her into action. She twisted from his grip and sprinted out into the yard. He followed her.

"Get away from me!" Kim screamed. The wind blew the words back into her face.

She broke into a run, tripped and fell to her knees. Selby came up, put an arm around her waist and pulled her to him. She suddenly realized his arm sling was gone and he was using both hands.

"You're hurting me, Selby! Git yer dirty hands off me, you sonofabitch!"

Selby laughed, grinning insanely as he dragged her across the yard towards the bunkhouse. Kim twisted and kicked at him. He stopped once to slam his fist hard against her jaw. She went slack in his arms. He hoisted her over his shoulder and trudged towards the bunkhouse.

Once in the bunkhouse he laid her out on a cot and stood staring down at her with intense eyes. A crazy fire seemed to blaze in them. He shook her and slapped her face until she came to.

"Wake up, little darlin'!" Selby chuckled. "It's jest us two on our honeymoon!" He let out with a high-pitched, insane cackle.

"Your arm!" she said, pointing.

Selby smiled and flexed his left arm. "Heck, it's jest fine, darling.'"

"But, you were shot!"

"Nope. Never was. After I kilt old Ed, I figured I'd put the blame on Jorth. It worked out pretty good, don't ya think?"

"So Jorth wasn't stealin' our cattle?"

"Nope. It was jest me, Smears an' Medford."

"I'll tell my mother!"

"No, ya won't," Selby said.

He reached under the bunk and pulled out a lariat. When Kim saw it she sat up and struck out, raking her nails across his left cheek. Selby groaned in pain, dropped the rope and felt his face. It was all bloody.

Kim twisted sideways and jumped up. She glared at Selby for a moment then ran for the door. As she went by Selby, he tackled her and slammed her back down onto the cot. She struggled as he wound the rope around her body. When it was finished she lay still, unable to move.

Selby wiped the blood from his face with his bandana.

Kim softened. "Why, Frank? Why? What did we ever do ta you?"

"Nothin', little darlin'," Selby said smiling. "It's jest me. It's the way I am. I've done stuff like this before."

"You gonna kill me?"

"When I'm ready, sure. After I kill the old man."

"You're crazy!"

"Sure. Crazy as a loon. But nobody knows it."

"They'll find out."

"Nope. They'll think Jorth had a hand in it. An' I won't even be here. I'll be miles away when the storm clears. I'll go up to Nebraska and do the same thing. It's easy. People are stupid. I always get away with it."

Selby stood up.

"Where are you going?" Kim asked. She knew the answer even before she spoke. "No, Frank, please. He's just a harmless old man. Don't hurt him, please!"

Selby stopped for a moment to look back.

"When I'm finished with Gran'paw and yer lover boy upstairs, I'll show ya how a real man makes love, little girl."

"I don't think so, Selby!"

Selby spun around at the sound of the voice.

McClain was standing in the doorway. He held one hand over his wound and leaned against the doorframe for support. He looked pale and weak. The wound was bleeding again.

"Thanks fer comin', McClain," Selby chuckled. "It makes it a lot easier."

"Was that you back on the road that night?" McClain asked. His voice was unsteady. He stepped further inside the room and dropped his right hand down by his gun.

"Yeah. I missed you then, but I won't this time."

Both men drew and fired at the same time. Selby's shot took McClain low in the chest. McClain's shot took Selby in the neck. He clasped a hand to his throat as blood shot from the main artery. He sat on the cot across from Kim and pointed his gun at her.

McClain shot him twice more. Selby tumbled over and was dead before he hit the floor.

McClain walked slowly over to where Kim lay. He sat on the cot, got out his boot knife and cut the rope in several places. Kim got loose and sat up. McClain dropped the boot knife. His eyes didn't seem to see her. His chest was now all bloody like his side. He hardly breathed.

"Lay down," Kim said.

She started to cry as she helped McClain down on the cot. She knew he was dying. His handsome face looked like a little boy's, so pale and innocent. He was sweating. He let out a low groan.

"Oh, God!" Kim cried.

"Would you have a kiss for a dying cowboy?" McClain asked. He tried to smile.

"Oh, yes" Kim said, wiping her eyes to clear them. "As many as ya want!"

She kissed his lips but they didn't respond. She knew then that he had gone far away and would never be back again.

9.

Fran finished telling the story.

"The next morning Jared saw where Ed Nealy had taken a stone and scratched Selby's name into the rock floor after Selby had shot him." Fran said. "So that was when we decided to come back as soon as we could."

They were sitting and talking on the front porch of the farmhouse. Virgil McClain was buried out back in the Darnell family's burial plot and Selby was buried in a lonely spot near a hill behind the barn.

The devil wind had calmed down some.

As for the yard, it looked as if it had been swept clean by a giant broom. The only signs of the storm were the small, telltale drifts of silt here and there. Also, the top section of the windmill was lying on the ground next to the corral.

"I think Selby and Smears were working together. Selby was stealing from the Diamond D and Smears was stealing from the Circle J. They probably had buyers in Ellsworth."

"I never did trust thet polecat!" old Seth Darnell growled.

Fran sighed, weary from everything. The past few days had been trying.

"Frank Selby was a strange man," she mused.

"He was crazy as a loon," Kim said.

"It's an old trick," Seth Darnell said, stroking his chin and grinning. "Ya play one side agin the other. Rustle cattle from both sides ta get them fightin' over it. It's a trick as old as the hills."

"Maybe my husband found out what Selby was up to, so Selby killed him," Fran said. "Then he killed Ed Nealy later." She paused to think a moment. "And here I was blaming Jorth."

"That's what Selby and Smears both wanted. I bet if Jorth looks, he'll find his cattle just like we found yours," Jared said.

"I was wrong about Bill all along," Fran said, then corrected herself. "I mean, Mr. Jorth."

Kim got up and walked down the porch steps into the yard.

"I'm goin' up ta see Mr. McClain," she said and walked around the house out of sight.

Fran sighed. "She's been going up there every day. I think she really liked Mr. McClain." She looked sad. "I miss him already, myself."

"So do I," Jared said. "He was a real cowboy."

"Wal, they don't make 'em like they used to," old Seth said. "We had real cowboys back in my day. Ya didn't dare lay hands on a woman, a horse or a cow when I was a young cowpoke."

Fran chuckled. "Of course, Dad. Of course."

"So, whatta ya gonna do about them beeves ya found up north?" Fran's father asked.

"What do you think we should do, Dad?"

The old man pondered the returned question for a moment.

"Well, there ain't no grass around these parts yet, so ya can't move 'em down here, thet's fer sure. If a good rain comes along there might be grass in a month or so. It does grow faster now than it used ta."

Fran and Jared chuckled.

79

"Sure it does, Dad. Sure it does."

They saw a buckboard coming slowly along the road in their direction. It rolled past the stand of pines and up to the opening in the fence and stopped. It was Mr. Carter, manager of the Cattlemen's Savings and Loan. He sat alone on the bench seat.

"Good day, Mrs. Darnell," Carter said, tipping his hat.

"Good day, Mr. Carter. What can I do for you?"

"I came to tell you to disregard that thirty-day notice I gave you, ma'am," Mr. Carter said.

"Why is that, Mr. Carter? I have the money now."

"Well, you can use your money for something else, Mrs. Darnell. It seems a secret male admirer of yours has paid off the entire balance on your mortgage."

"I don't know of anyone who would do that, Mr. Carter," Fran said. "There must be some mistake."

Mr. Carter got down from the buckboard and walked over to the porch. Fran stood up and met him. The man took a piece of paper from his coat pocket and handed it to Fran.

"What's this?" she asked.

"It's the deed to your property," he replied.

For a moment the woman wasn't sure she had heard right. "The deed?"

"Yes, ma'am. The deed. Free and clear."

"Is this a joke?"

"No, ma'am, it's not a joke."

"Who did this?"

"I'm not at liberty to say, ma'am."

Fran stared at the piece of paper in her hand. She was dazed. Perhaps she was dreaming or going out of her mind.

"Did you say this is the deed to the Diamond D, Mr. Carter?"

"I did and it is."

"Alright, then. Thank you, sir."

Mr. Carter chuckled. "Don't thank me, Mrs. Darnell. Thank...well, never mind. I'm not allowed to reveal his name."

"Then how can I thank him if you won't tell me who he is?"

"That is a problem, isn't it, ma'am?" Mr. Carter took off his hat and scratched his baldhead. "I'll tell you what, and don't say I said this, but Mr. Jorth is throwing a shindig out at his ranch in two weeks. He wants you to come. Ask him about it. Good day, Mrs. Darnell."

The bank man got back on the buckboard and tipped his hat again. He looked up at the sky.

"I think we'll be having rain soon." He snapped the reins and rode away.

"He's crazy. It ain't gonna rain," Seth chuckled.

Fran walked back up on the porch and handed the piece of paper to Jared.

"Is this what he said it is?" she asked.

Jared unfolded the paper and looked it over, then handed it back.

"It is, ma'am," Jared chuckled. "It's exactly what he said it is."

"Praise be to God!" Fran said. A second later she added, "And praise be to Bill, I mean, Mr. Jorth."

She stared hard at the piece of paper in her hand. It was just a little scrap of paper with some words and some signatures on it. Yet it contained all the power and strength of an army.

Kim came running around the house, all excited.

"What's wrong, darlin'?"

"I saw lightning in the northwest! And there are clouds a-comin' this way."

"Show me, baby!"

Fran and Jared rushed down into the yard. Kim pointed toward the northwest horizon. Miles away they saw the bank of gray clouds being split open by lightning. It was too far away for the sound of thunder to reach them.

Kim grabbed her mother and whirled her around.

"Let's do a rain dance, Momma!"

And they did.

10.

Early in the morning of the next day it began to rain in the Salisbury area. It was a good, solid rain that moved slowly in a wide path. By nightfall it had dropped four inches on the parched land. It continued falling all that night and well into the next day. Turtles came out of their holes and frogs appeared by the hundreds. In six days, buds sprouted from the birches, aspens and cottonwood trees.

Lightning strikes shattered and split the dead trees but left the healthy ones to drink and thrive. Sometimes the rain slacked off and the clouds parted to let the sun in to nurture the dormant seeds of the wild rye, brome sedge and bluestem. Soon the seedlings poked their tiny heads through the now soaked earth and reached for the sky. The natural rhythm of the plains was resurrected like Lazarus rising from the dead.

One day, young Kim Darnell ran barefoot in the yard in a chemise. She stretched her arms and tilted her head back to catch the drops in her mouth. Her hair hung down behind her shoulders, dripping and heavy with rain. She ran about stomping in the puddles.

Running over to the corral, she slipped under the fence and hugged and kissed Wildfire. She led him out of the corral and leaped upon his back. Grabbing a handful of his mane, she tapped his barrel with her bare feet and the great animal shot forward into a sprint. Kim hung on, screaming for joy. They dashed out of the yard and across the greening field. Half an hour later they returned, exhausted and soaked. She put him in the corral again and went stomping in more puddles.

Old Seth rolled his wheelchair out on the porch to watch. He looked concerned. Fran came out carrying a towel.

"You better watch out, girl!" Seth hollered down at Kim. "If'n one of them fire sticks hit you, you'll light up like a bonfire! It'll set yer hair on fire!"

By then Kim was exhausted. She ran into her mother's arms to get dried off.

"Yer mother use ta do that very same thing when she was young," the old man said, as if boasting.

"Of course I did," Fran said.

Jared, who had watched from the bunkhouse, rushed out across the yard and up on the porch. He sat down next to the old man. Seth looked at him.

"Summer is almost over," the old man said. "It'll be fall soon. We'll have ta plan fer winter. Stock up the root cellar an' all."

Jared nodded.

"If'n the birds head south early this year or the sheep grow heavy coats or beavers cut down more wood, watch out!"

"What's that mean, Gran'paw?" Kim asked.

"It means a darn cold winter is what it means. Heck, everybody knows thet, girl."

"Oh, Gran'paw," Kim replied, "you sure kin tell some tall tales." She took the towel from her mother.

Fran sat down beside Jared.

"Isn't this wonderful?" she said. "If it keeps up like this, we'll have good graze in a month."

"I hope it stops long enough ta go to the barn dance," Kim said.

"Mr. Jared," Fran said, "do you have a jacket? If not, you can wear one of my husband's."

"Alright, ma'am, that would be nice."

That Friday afternoon the rain stopped and they got ready to go to the barn dance at the Circle J. Fran and Kim wore simple dresses and low shoes for dancing.

"There's ham, beans and biscuits in the larder and the coffee pot is full, Dad," Fran said. "We won't be gone all that long."

"I'll be jest fine," old Seth said. "You three run along an' have a good time."

They went outside to where the buckboard was waiting in the yard. Fran's father sat on the porch in his wheelchair watching as Fran and Kim climbed up and rode out with Jared handling the reins. The girls turned and waved at him and Seth waved back.

Two hours later they rode into the yard of the Circle J farmhouse.

Jared suddenly realized how big the Circle J was. Everything was bigger here, the two-story, white-washed clapboard house, the corral with over fifty horses, the towering windmill, the two huge barns and bunkhouse. There was an opening under one side of the house that led to a root cellar. There were chicken coops and rabbit hutches. Chickens and ducks were on the loose, along with dogs and cats.

Of the two barns, one was functional while the other was used for meetings and social gatherings, much like a Grange Hall.

"Wow!" Kim said. "Look at all those buckboards! There must be over a thousand people here!"

The yard was packed with horses, buckboards and carriages of different sizes, including carryalls. They found a rare, open spot outside in a field where they tied the horse to a tree and made their way back to the barn.

They could hear music as they walked into the yard. In the barn Marshal Landry stopped them.

"Howdy, folks."

He had Jared hang his gunbelt from a peg on the wall.

There were benches along two opposite walls. Three musicians stood on a plank platform near the back wall. One played a banjo, one a violin and one a mouth harp. They played a lively tune while couples danced in the open area between the benches.

Multi-colored Japanese lanterns hung from the rafters. Red and blue ribbons dangled in between. The updraft stirred them so that they waved down at the dancers.

There was a long plank table to the right of the entrance. It was piled high with all kinds of sliced meats, boiled eggs, pickles and biscuits. Combined with this were baskets of apples, pears and plums and bowls of cider and fruit punch.

The guests wishing stronger drink brought their own.

Children ran around between the benches and across the dance floor, sometimes tripping over the dancers. Some of the older children danced beside their elders.

Men were gathered in small groups drinking from pintsized bottles of whiskey as they smoked. Their wives sat in little pods discussing the latest gossip.

Bill Jorth came from somewhere.

"Fran," he said. "I'm so glad you could come."

"Thank you for inviting me, William."

"I was afraid you wouldn't come."

"Well, as you can see, I did," Fran said.

Jared was surprised by how familiar they were with one another. It was if they were old friends meeting again after being apart for a few years.

Jorth and Fran stared into each other's eyes.

"I believe this is our dance, Fran."

"I do believe it is, William."

Jorth took Fran Darnell's hand and led her out onto the dance floor to join the other dancers. People stared from the benches. Some chattered and some smiled.

A young cowboy came over and asked Kim to dance. She looked at Jared.

"Go dance, Miss Kim," he said.

She left with the young man and Jared went over to the table and filled a glass with cider. He took it over to a bench in a far corner and sat down to drink. Two men walked over to him. On was tall and skinny, the other short and stocky.

"Are you the one called Jared?" the tall one asked.

"Yep, that's me, cowboy," Jared replied.

"We'd like to talk to you outside."

Jared chuckled. "Is it about Medford and Smears?"

"Yep," the short one said. "You guessed it."

"You were pards, right?"

"We both were," the tall one said.

Jared nodded. "Can't we let it ride?"

"Nope," the short one said.

"I'll tell you what," Jared said calmly. "Just walk away and I won't hurt either of you."

The two cowboys looked at each other and burst out laughing.

"What's so funny?" Jared asked, smiling.

"If we walk away, you won't hurt us? Is that what you just said?"

"Yep."

The tall one sneered. "How the hell you gonna hurt us, asshole?"

"Like this."

Jared tossed his drink in the tall one's eyes and slammed the glass against the side of his head. His eyes rolled up in his head and he collapsed in a heap on the floor.

Before the short, stocky cowboy could go for his gun, Jared drove his fist straight into his face, breaking his nose. He staggered and stepped back on wobbling legs, then shook the blow off. He roared like a bull and dove at Jared.

Jared danced to the right, sidestepping. The cowboy went past him and crashed into a group of men in suits, knocking two down. Their drinks went flying.

That made them angry.

Another Circle J man came from the shadows and threw a punch at Jared, catching him in the ribs. Jared grunted and went down on one knee. The attacker kicked out. Jared caught the boot and twisted it as hard as he could. Something snapped and the cowboy went down screaming.

As Jared got up, three more Circle J men came at him. Things looked bad until a man in a suit jumped in to help Jared. A few seconds later another suit came to help his friend. After that it was a free-for-all. Cowboys and suits tangled in a bruising fistfight. Jared and a man in a blue suit stood back to back, slugging it out with Jorth's men.

The fight spread to the dance floor. Women and children went screaming for the doors. Some women stayed to do battle alongside their men. No one had any idea what the fight was about. Some didn't care. After a long, brutal drought, this was like a safety valve letting off steam.

There was a gunshot and everyone froze.

"Everybody sit the hell down," Marshal Landry commanded. Bill Jorth was standing next to him looking worried.

The crowd slowly disengaged. Some people sat down to nurse their wounds and others headed for the punch bowl.

But the fight was over.

The coat Jared wore was half torn off his back. He had a bruised right cheek and a cut on his chin. He limped over to the cider bowl holding his ribs. As he filled a glass, the two Circle J cowboys came over to him.

"This ain't over," the tall one said.

They poured themselves a glass of cider and walked over to join their buddies. Occasionally they looked over at Jared. There was no doubt they were discussing him.

Some people left early but most didn't. The music started up again and dancers took to the floor. Kim came over with a boy in tow and gawked at Jared. She laughed.

"Looks like you took a good whippin', Mr. Jared."

"Yeah, I reckon I did, Kim," Jared replied.

Kim dragged the boy away onto the dance floor. Jared took his glass of cider over to a dark corner and sat down.

Jared saw Fran Darnell and Bill Jorth dancing. It was a waltz and he held her close. They looked good together. He wanted to feel good about them but he couldn't. Not with what he knew.

It was dark when they started back to the Diamond D.

"I wonder how the fight got started, Mr. Jared?" Fran asked.

"I have no idea, ma'am," Jared replied. She couldn't see him smiling in the darkness.

It was late when they got back to the Diamond D. There were no lights in the windows.

"Gran'paw musta fell asleep in his chair agin," Kim chuckled.

She and her mother dismounted.

"I'll take care of the horse," Jared said. He grabbed its harness.

The women went into the house. Jared sat there a moment then drove the buckboard down to the barn.

He had just finished unhitching the buckboard when a horrible whining sound came from the ranch house. Jared hesitated a moment then rushed out into the yard. There was a light on in the kitchen now and he ran towards it. Seconds later he stood beside Kim and her mother.

Old Seth Darnell was slumped back in his wheel chair with a piece of pie in his lap.

He wasn't breathing.

11.

While Jared dug the grave, Fran and Kim took the buckboard into Salisbury to buy a ready-made casket from the undertaker there. They brought it back to the Diamond D and Fran lined it with a brown flannel bedspread. Kim helped them lift old Seth in and Jared nailed the top on. When that was finished, they loaded it on the buckboard and took it out to the small burial plot behind the ranch house.

After they lowered the casket into the ground, Fran read from the family Bible. Kim read a poem and Jared filled the hole in. He placed a crude cross on it with Seth Darnell's name and dates of birth and death.

A few days later, Fran found Jared brushing down his horse in the barn. She walked up to him.

"Mr. Jared, can I talk to you?"

"Sure," Jared said quickly.

"It's about Bill Jorth."

"Oh? What about him, ma'am?"

She hesitated a moment. "He's interested in me."

"I see," Jared replied. He wondered why she was telling him this. He asked anyway. "And you?"

"I'm going with it. I'm going to let it happen."

Jared chuckled. "Thanks for telling me, ma'am, but it's none of my business, is it?"

"I want you to ramrod the Circle J when it happens."

"What about the Diamond D?"

"Mr. Jorth will handle the sale for me."

Jared nodded. "I see." He paused for a moment. "I'll have to think on it, ma'am."

"Alright. There's no rush," Fran said. "I'll see you get paid double wages." She started to walk away but stopped and came back.

"There is something else. It's about Kim." Jared stopped brushing the horse to listen. "You gave her Mr. McClain's horse and all his gear."

"Yes. She said she wanted it to remember him by."

"I discovered she sleeps with his gunbelt and gun. She even has a little shrine where she puts it during the day. Mr. McClain's hat is there, too."

"I see."

"She said as long as McClain's body is here on the Diamond D she'll never leave it."

Jared nodded.

"I talked to her but she won't listen," Fran said. "Maybe you could try."

"Alright, ma'am."

"Perhaps now would be a good time. She won't leave her room."

Jared nodded, put away the brush and followed Fran into the ranch house. They stood in the kitchen. He felt awkward.

"Would you like a cup of coffee, first, before you go up?" she asked.

"Thank you, no," Jared said. He chuckled nervously. "I never did this before."

"Please." Her eyes were moist.

"Alright," Jared said.

He went upstairs to Kim's room and knocked softly on the door. There was no answer so he knocked again.

"Go away, Momma!"

Jared cleared his throat. "It's me, Miss Kim." There was a moment of silence. "Can I talk to you?"

"No" Then, "Well, wait a moment." He heard the bed covers rustle inside. "Alright, you can come in now."

Jared opened the door and went in with his hat in his hand. Kim lay on the bed fully dressed. Jared saw the shrine to McClain over in the corner on a small table. There was a candle there but it wasn't lit now.

"Can I sit, Miss Kim?"

She nodded and he sat carefully on the edge of the bed. He saw where she had tried to hide McClain's gunbelt under her pillow. A part of it stuck out.

"What do you want, Mr. Jared?"

"You really miss McClain, don't you?"

"Yes. He loved me. I love him and I always will."

"He's dead. It's a bad love, Kim."

"No it isn't. Elaine did it." Kim replied.

"Elaine?" For a moment Jared was confused. "A friend of yours?"

"No. She guarded Lancelot's shield. She lived in a tower. Lancelot loved her jest as Mr. McClain loved me."

Jared suddenly knew what she meant. She was the fair Elaine guarding brave Lancelot's shield.

"King Arthur?"

Kim nodded.

"That was a fairy tale, Kim. It wasn't real."

Suddenly the girl began to sob.

"You should have seen him, Mr. Jared. Mr. McClain was wonderful. He stood there in thet doorway like a knight! He was fearless, even though wounded! He faced thet horrible dragon Selby and slayed him right before my eyes."

She cried harder, her body shaking, her hands over her eyes to hold back the flood of tears. She spoke haltingly, catching her breath between words.

"Oh, God! He died fer me! If it wasn't fer me, he would still be alive! How can I not love him? He's my brave knight!"

Jared nodded. He could feel the girl's anguish and pain. McClain had gotten close to him too, with his perpetual smile and devil-may-care ways. He had been a free soul. One of God's special children.

"Miss Kim," Jared said, "every cowboy has a trail to ride. He has to follow it wherever it takes him. Sometimes it's a long trail and sometime it's short. It has a beginning and an end. McClain's trail ended at your feet. Thank God it ended the way it did, for your mother's sake."

Kim let out a big sigh and nodded.

"I'm not leaving the Diamond D."

Jared smiled and nodded. "I'll talk to your mother. Maybe we can figure something out."

Kim brightened up. "Oh, would you, please?"

"Yes."

Suddenly the girl leaned in and gave him a hug. Jared went back down to the kitchen for a cup of coffee.

"How did it go?" Fran asked.

Jared chuckled. "I lost. She won."

"I don't understand."

"Ma'am, I reckon that's the problem. We didn't understand." Jared explained about Lancelot's shield.

"I see," Fran said. "What do you suggest?"

Jared sipped his coffee thinking about what to say.

"Well," he finally responded, "why not keep the Diamond D for a while? Leave Miss Kim here to help run it. Mr. Jorth can hire some good cowboys to handle the new herd. In the meantime, maybe Kim will spot another McClain in the bunch of good-looking cowpokes."

"That might work, Mr. Jared," Fran said. "But what about you ramrodding the Circle J?"

"I'd rather stay here for a while."

"A while?"

Jared smiled. "I get a bad case of the wanders every so often, if you know what I mean."

Fran chuckled. "No. Women usually don't catch that. It's strictly a cowboy's sickness, thank God."

12.

Jared had a secret and it ate at him like a hungry animal. It was a secret that could tear Fran Darnell and Bill Jorth apart. He realized that he had waited too long, that he should have told her days ago, at the very beginning when he first learned it. But he had waited, not wanting to make her life more complicated than it was.

Had he known how things were going to go between her and Jorth, he would have told her.

Bill Jorth had killed her husband.

That was what Ron Medford had whispered in his ear just before he died. At first Jared didn't believe it. Maybe Medford was trying to make trouble and had lied. But, maybe again, he hadn't, and that was the pickle Jared was in.

In any case, he couldn't just walk up to Fran and say, "The man you're going to marry killed your husband!" No, he couldn't do that but he had to.

So, Jared decided to go into town.

He told Fran he was going to Dobson's Mercantile for more bullets and left late in the morning. He rode into town an hour later, tied up at the jailhouse and went in. The marshal was sitting at his desk doing some paperwork.

"Howdy, Mr. Jared," the crusty old man said. "Come ta confess, have ya?"

Jared looked wide-eyed for a moment.

"Confess? To what? I didn't do anything."

The marshal chuckled. "Like the dickens, ya didn't. It was you who started thet fight out at Jorth's place. I saw the whole thing."

Jared shrugged "I had no choice. It was either shoot or fight, so I figured I'd fight."

"Good choice," the marshal replied. "Sit down, sonny. What brings you here?"

Jared sat in a chair next to the marshal's desk.

"You remember that night when McClain and I were braced by Smears and Medford?"

"Yeah, what about it?"

"Do you remember me bending over Medford?"

"Yeah. I was wonderin' what thet was all about. You finally goin' ta tell me, are ya?"

Jared nodded. "He told me that Bill Jorth killed Fran Darnell's husband."

"He said Bill Jorth killed Tim Darnell?"

"Those were his exact words," Jared replied.

The old marshal whistled and stroked his stubbly chin.

"Have you told Mrs. Darnell?"

"No. I can't."

"Why not?"

"Jorth is interested in her. They're gonna get married."

The marshal pondered the problem.

"It's well known that Tim Darnell and Bill Jorth hated each other."

"Why?"

"She never told you?"

"No. Why should she?"

"Her an' Jorth were close before Tim Darnell came along an' fancy-talked her into marryin' him."

"I never knew that."

"Well yer not from here," the marshal said, "so how could ya know?"

Jared nodded and fell quiet for a time.

"Give me a piece of paper and something to write with," the cowboy said.

"What fer?"

"Because I'm asking."

"Yer askin' fer trouble," The marshal said grudgingly. He got pencil and paper from his desk and gave them to Jared. "An' yer puttin' me in a bad spot, too."

"It's my ass as well," Jared said and started writing.

In half an hour he was finished. He handed the statement to the marshal. The old lawman looked it over and nodded. He sighed, folded the paper and stuck it in his vest pocket.

He stood up. "Hell, I was gonna retire soon, anyway, sonny. You kin have my job, if we survive this mess yer a-makin'."

Jared smiled. "No, thanks."

"Well, I ain't lettin' ya off thet easy, sonny."

The marshal got a deputy badge from his desk.

"Here, pin this on. Yer a deputy."

"Now wait a minute, Marshal!" Jared said.

"Pin it on or we ain't goin' out there."

Jared pinned on the badge.

They mounted up and headed out for the Circle J Ranch. In two hours they rode into the yard, tied up at the fence and walked the rest of the way to the house. They found Jorth in his study talking to the tall, slim cowboy that Jared had fought with.

"Wait outside, Lou," Jorth said. Lou gave Jared a dirty look and left. Jorth waited a moment. "What brings you way out here, Ned?"

The marshal handed the rancher Jared's statement. Jorth opened the paper and looked at it for a moment. He shrugged and smiled.

"You don't believe this, do you, Ned?"

"It don't matter what I believe, Bill," the marshal replied. "It's fer the jury ta decide."

Jorth laughed. "You can't be serious, Ned."

"I've got no choice, Bill."

"We've been friends for a long time, Ned."

"This ain't got nothin' ta do with friendship, Bill. It's about the law. Procedure is what it's all about. You'll get a fair trial. You'll likely be found not guilty, and you kin go home."

"So, you're going to put me in jail in Salisbury? And let the town look in on me like I was some freak?"

"Jest until the trial, Bill."

Jorth smiled. "Lou!"

Lou stood in the doorway staring in.

"Lou, go get Gil, Stan and Wally. Be quick."

"Yes sir, Mr. Jorth." Lou ran off.

Marshal Landry held up a hand, as if pleading for mercy.

"Now. Take it easy, Bill."

Jorth sneered.

"You're forgetting, I made you marshal, Ned. You were just a town drunk looking for work when I picked you out of the gutter and put a badge on you. You ungrateful bastard!"

The old man seemed to shrink in on himself. The words crushed him.

"Now don't get mad, Bill!"

"You let that badge go to your head, old man," Jorth said scornfully. "I guess I'll have to put you in your place."

Lou came running back with Gil, Stan and Wally, all big men wearing guns.

"The marshal and his deputy was just leaving, boys," Jorth said. "Escort them off the Circle J. Take the special road. The one over by the quicksand pit."

"Gil, you an' Stan git their irons," Lou said. After that was done he growled, "Tie 'em both up and put 'em in the buckboard."

When they had left and the yard was cleared of horses, Jorth sat at his desk looking worried. That damn Medford had ratted on him just before he died, the sonofabitch. May he rot in hell.

Jorth had just started back at the paperwork on his desk when he heard a buckboard pull up into the yard.

He got up and walked to the door just as Fran Darnell came up the porch steps. He heaved a sigh of relief and went to her. They kissed and he brought her into the house.

"Have a seat, darling," he said.

Fran took a chair facing Jorth's desk. He took a chair behind it.

"I came to give you my answer, Bill," Fran said smiling. She seemed anxious and happy.

"I hope it's the one I want, darling."

"It is. Yes."

Jorth quickly got up and ran around to Fran. She stood up. They embraced and kissed again.

"About selling the Diamond D," Fran said. "Mr. Jared had something else in mind."

"Oh, really? What is that?"

Fran explained the plan to keep the Diamond D for a while before selling it off.

"That was very clever of Mr. Jared. When I see him again I'll have to shake his hand and compliment him."

The way he said it didn't sound like a compliment at all.

13.

The cowboy named Gil, the short and stocky one, drove the buckboard while Lou, Stan and Wally rode alongside. They followed a trail through a large pine forest.

Lou smiled down at where the marshal and Jared lay in the back of the flatbed wagon with their hands and feet tied.

"You did me a big favor by killin' off Smears and Medford, Jared," Lou chuckled. "You made me ramrod."

"Then you owe me a favor, Lou," Jared said.

"Naw. It don't work thet way, Jared."

"Why not? Hell, just cut me lose. You can still kill the old man. I'll ride out and keep going."

"Sure you will." Lou laughed. "You hear thet boys? He wants us ta kill the old buzzard then spring him loose! Ain't that nice?"

Gil, Stan and Wally laughed.

"I guess he thinks we're dumb," Wally chortled.

"Yeah," Stan said.

"Well, it was worth a try," Jared chuckled.

His mind raced. He was scared. His heart was thumping in his chest. Dying in a quicksand hole was not as exciting as shooting it out. With a gun you had a chance.

"Say, Lou," Jared said calmly. "Smears was pretty fast on the draw but my pard beat him."

"Yeah, and you beat Medford. He was slow as a snail."

"Oh, I could have beat Smears, too, I think," Jared said.

"I don't think so," Lou returned quickly. "I was on the Sagebrush Saloon porch that day. You didn't look all that fast to me."

"I went slow on Medford," Jared said. "I let him get his gun out before I shot him."

The cowboys chuckled.

"Bullshit!" Stan said.

"No bullshit," Jared said.

"You think yer fast, huh?" Wally asked.

"I'm damn fast," Jared said.

"You think you could beat Lou?"

Lou glared at Wally.

"Shut up," Lou hissed.

"Hell, Lou, you kin take this loudmouth," Wally went on. He paused a moment. "I mean, can't ya?"

"I said shut yer trap!" Lou shouted.

For a moment no one said anything. Then Stan spoke.

"It sounds like yer afraid of Jared, Lou," Stan said.

"I ain't afraid of nobody!" Lou's feathers were ruffled.

"Say," Stan said, "I got an idea. Let's do it like they did thet day at the Sagebrush."

"What the hell are you talkin' about?" Lou asked.

"Us four against them two," Stan explained. "We have us a shootout."

"Are you crazy?" Lou asked.

"Hell, no! We shoot them two assholes all to ribbons and then toss 'em into the quicksand."

"Come on, Lou, loosen up," Wally said. "It ain't no fun jest tossin' them in all trussed up like this. Be a sport."

Lou inhaled deeply, exhaled, and then chuckled.

"Hell, why not. We're gonna kill 'em one way or another, anyway. Later we kin tell the boss how we did it. He'll git a big kick out of it."

They talked about how much fun they were going to have until they came up to a small opening in the pines. They stopped, dismounted and smoked. Stan got a bottle from his saddlebag and they drank and talked some more.

"Damn nice weather," Gil noted. "Sure glad thet damn dry spell is over." They all nodded in agreement.

"Damn good whiskey, Stan," Wally said.

Finally, the Circle J men untied Jared and the old man. The two climbed down on cramped legs, hardly able to stand up.

"Can we have a minute?" Marshal Landry asked. "My darn legs are asleep."

"Sure, ol' man," Lou said. They all took a long, final pull on the bottle. It was now empty. Wally tossed it into the quicksand pit. Jared and the marshal stood watching it sink slowly out of sight.

Jared slapped his legs and stomped his feet. He looked up. There were crows watching in the pines. He smiled.

"Give 'em back their irons, Gil," Lou said.

There wasn't much room to spread out, twenty feet at the most. Jared looked at the old man. The marshal winked at him as if to say not to worry.

"So, you were the town drunk, huh, Marshal?" Jared asked as he massaged his wrist to get the circulation back.

"Yeah, but once I was somebody else," the marshal answered.

"Yeah? Who were you?"

"When I was yer age I was the Wahoo Kid, from Nebrasky."

"Jesus!" Jared said. "You were a legend!"

"I'm still a legend," the old man said, grinning.

Without saying a word, the old marshal turned to face the four men. Jared turned with him.

"Draw, you sidewinders!" the old man shouted. The crows above in the pines scattered in a rush of wings.

The old man's gun was out first and barking. Lou and Gil, on the left facing the marshal, were hit in the chest as they fired back. They both looked surprised and tried to fan off a second shot but were drilled again between the eyes. Their heads snapped back as if smacked by a sledgehammer, and their legs turned to rubber. They hit the ground hard.

Jared went into a crouch and fanned off four quick shots. Stan took a bullet in the belly and in the heart. Wally took two in the heart. Both cowboys dropped like a rock, Stan on his back and Wally on his face.

Jared felt a burning in his left arm. He stood up and put his hand there. It came away bloody.

"I got hit, too," the marshal chuckled. "In the hat!" He walked over and picked his hat up. It had a bullet hole high up in the crown.

Jared removed his bandana. The marshal tied it around his arm.

"Hurt bad?" the marshal asked.

"No," Jared said. "Damn, you're fast."

"I was faster once," the old lawman said. He looked at the bodies. "Let's give these sidewinders back ta Jorth."

14.

Jorth got a bottle of brandy from his kitchen larder and brought it and two glasses into his study.

"Let us toast, Fran," he said cheerfully. "To us, darling. May we be together forever."

Jorth poured the drinks. They stood facing each other.

"To us and forever," Fran said.

After touching their glasses, they drank.

"This brandy is delicious, William," Fran said.

"Yes, it is. Vintage 1875. Ten years old."

They put their glasses on the desk and embraced.

"I'll make you happy, Francine," Jorth said. "I would have married you many years ago if Tim hadn't come along."

"That's all in the past now," Fran said. "We'll start over again." She laughed softly. "You know, at one time I thought that you were responsible for Tim's death."

For a second Jorth's eyes flickered cold. He recovered and smiled.

"Whatever gave you that idea?"

"My father. He also had Kim convinced that you had Tim killed, or did it yourself." She laughed. "I see now how silly that was."

"Let's not think about that, Francine," Jorth said quickly.

There was the distant sound of horses. It got gradually closer until a buckboard could be heard coming into the yard. Jorth stepped away from Fran and went to the door. He opened it and looked out. Fran came up beside him.

She saw the two men in the buckboard and the horses tied behind it.

"Why, it's the Marshal and Jared!" Fran cried.

Fran rushed past Jorth and down into the yard before he could stop her. She ran up to the buckboard and stared at the bodies.

"My God! What happened?"

"It's a long story, ma'am," Jared said.

He and the marshal climbed down.

118

"Is Bill Jorth in there, ma'am?" the marshal asked.

"Why, yes, he is."

The marshal nodded, walked over to the porch steps and stopped. He looked up at the open door.

"Bill Jorth," Marshal Landry yelled, "you're under arrest for murder and attempted murder! Come out and surrender to the law!"

Fran stared at Jared. She looked lost and confused.

"What's going on, Mr. Jared? I don't understand!"

"I can't tell you right now, ma'am. Please stay here." Jared said and walked over beside the marshal.

"Come on out here, Jorth. I know yer in there!"

A minute passed. There was no answer.

"I'm a comin' in ta git ya, Bill!"

"One moment, Ned!" Jorth called out. "One moment!"

They heard footsteps and some noise. Then a gun went off inside the house. Something heavy fell on the floor.

"Oh, God!" Fran groaned. She made to run towards the house. Jared grabbed her arm and held her. She screamed, "Bill darling!"

"Let her go," the marshal said.

Jared nodded and let go of Fran's arm. She disappeared into the house. Seconds later they heard her crying. A cowboy came out of the bunkhouse.

"Where's the others?" the marshal asked.

"Out on the range," the cowboy said, rubbing his eyes. He had just woken up. "I got a sick day off." He saw the dead bodies. "Christ Almighty! What happened?"

"It's a long story," the marshal said. "Go back to sleep, sonny."

The cowboy went back into the bunkhouse.

Jared waited until Fran finally came out of the house. Her face was red from crying.

"Why?" she asked, staring at the marshal.

The old man looked at Jared for help.

"I'll tell you on the way home, ma'am," Jared said.

He tied his horse to the back of her buckboard and helped her up. He got in beside her. The marshal looked at them and nodded. Jared snapped the reins and headed for the Diamond D.

The old marshal stood alone in the yard watching the buckboard go out of sight. He looked around. Finally, he shook his head and sighed. He had known Bill Jorth a long time. Jorth had been good to him.

"Goddamn the law!" the marshal said under his breath.

He walked up the porch steps into the house to see the body of his old friend.

15.

Jared didn't know how to tell Fran so it would soften the blow. She had suffered enough with the death of her husband and, lately, her father. And now her promising future had exploded in seconds. It would be a bitter pill to swallow, knowing the truth.

"Why?" Fran asked, choking back tears.

"It looks like your father was right, ma'am."

"About what?"

"About the death of your husband."

"But he didn't really know. He was just guessing."

"Well, he was guessing right."

"How do you know?"

"Because Ron Medford told me before he died."

"I don't believe you."

"Why would I lie?"

She didn't answer.

"Why do you think Jorth killed himself?"

He knew that was the question she feared most. It was all the proof she needed. It answered the question for her.

She sobbed quietly for a while. Finally, she spoke.

"Bill and I were very close before Tim came along and swept me off my feet with his fancy talk. After Kim was born, Tim changed. And I began to see him for what he was, a lazy man who cared only about himself and not Kim or me."

She stopped a moment to collect her thoughts.

"When he was shot, I wasn't that sorry. I can't say I really loved him. I had to work hard to keep the ranch going. He was only in the way. I didn't want to lose the ranch. It had been in my family for a long time. All I cared about was Dad, Kim and the Diamond D. Nothing else really mattered."

Jared nodded.

"I can understand that, ma'am. I really can."

Suddenly Fran smiled and sniffed.

"Shucks, what am I crying for? Thanks to you, Mr. McClain and Mr. Jorth I still have my ranch and I'll soon have a herd, too."

"That's a good way to look at it, ma'am," Jared said. "I'll ramrod the Diamond D for you until it gets back on its feet."

"It'll take a long time, I'm afraid. We have less than a thousand head of beef."

"I think I know where we can get some more."

"Oh, where?"

"The ones Smears, Selby and Medford stole from you," Jared said. "I got a good idea they're stashed someplace on the Circle J. All I need is the Marshal to help me get 'em."

"I can ride as good as any cowboy," Fran said. "And so can Kim."

"Good," Jared said. "We'll make a move on the Circle J first thing tomorrow."

"Alright, Mr. Jared." Fran said. "But we'll have to take care of that arm of yours today."

When they got back to the Diamond D, Fran looked at Jared's arm.

"You're lucky. You just got kissed."

She cleaned and put a bandage on it.

Kim came down from upstairs. She had been crying again.

"I ain't leavin'," she said. "You can't make me!

"Nobody is leaving," Fran said. "We're staying here where we belong. With Mr. McClain."

Kim's eyes lit up. "Really?"

"Really," Fran said.

Kim rushed into her mother's arms and they hugged.

"What happened to Mr. Jared's arm?"

"It's a long story," Jared chuckled.

16.

Jared, Fran and Kim rode over to Jorth's ranch with the marshal to talk to the cowboys of the Circle J. It was a Friday and they were gathered in the bunkhouse.

"Men," Marshal Landry said, "Jorth had no kin. The Circle J is gonna be sold off to the highest bidder. That might take a while ta get done."

A good-looking young cowboy stood up smiling.

"So what yer sayin', Marshal, is we'd best go looking fer a job. Is thet it?"

"What's yer name, sonny?" the marshal asked.

"Ted. Ted Ramsey."

"Well, Mr. Ramsey, what I'm a-sayin' is, I'm afraid so. Unless ya wanna work fer nothin'."

The sound of grumbling rippled through the bunkhouse.

Jared stepped forward and cleared his throat for attention.

"Who the hell are you?" young Ramsey asked.

"I'm Clay Jared, ramrod of the Diamond D. This is Mrs. Darnell, owner, and her daughter Kim."

Young Ramsey got an eyeful of Kim Darnell. She stared boldly back at him. His goose was cooked right then and there. He stood gawking at her with a stupid smile on his face.

"The Diamond D is hiring," Jared said. "But we can only pay for six hands until the summer drive. Then we'll be at full swing and paying regular. Anybody want to sign on for the Diamond D brand, raise yer right hand."

Twenty hands went up. All young cowboys. They had never seen the likes of Kim Darnell and were anxious to get closer. Some didn't know their left hand from their right.

"Hell," one yelled, "I'll work fer free, if she'll give me a kiss!"

That brought lots of laughter.

"Miss Kim," Jared chuckled, "why don't you pick them out."

"My pleasure, Mr. Jared," Kim said smoothly.

Jared turned to the group of waiting cowhands.

"When the lady points at you, step over here."

Kim Darnell smiled and walked up to the anxious cowboys. She looked at Ramsey for a second then walked past him and up to the crowd. She pointed five times, then hesitated. Young Ramsey looked worried about being left out. Kim turned her back to him for a moment, then spoke.

"Alright, big mouth, you kin come."

A roar of laughter shot through the bunkhouse.

An hour later the Diamond D had its crew of wild, eager young blood anxious to ride the range and fight for the brand. Jared suggested they hire the cook now so they'd have one when they were up to full strength of fifteen hands.

Two days after they had settled in at the bunkhouse, Jared took them out on a quest to test his theory that Selby, Smears and Medford had stolen cattle from the Diamond D.

Seven days later it was proved to be right.

It took that many days of riding, camping out and looking through a telescope to locate them. It was young Ramsey who spotted the first strays, a mother with her calf coming out of a gulch. They looked well fed and healthy. The cowboys rode into the gulch and came out onto the same scene as Jared and Fran had at the north end of the Diamond D. There was a valley and a small lake surrounded by pines.

Selby, Smears and Medford had stashed over nine thousand head in there. It was their motherlode from which to sell off in small bunches to avoid suspicion. Over seven thousand of the cows had the Diamond D brand on them.

It took a week to get them all back on Diamond D land.

Jared and Fran talked one evening while drinking coffee on the porch. Kim and young Ramsey were walking up to the family burial plot.

"Those two are getting pretty close," Fran said.

"She'll tell him about McClain. Set the bar high for him."

"You think so?" Fran replied.

"Yeah," Jared said. "And that's good."

"Yes. I hope it works out for Kim. Better for her than what I had."

"You have her, and that's all that matters," Jared said. "Without her you'd be lonely, now that your father is gone. She'll fill the house with a son someday soon."

Fran looked at Jared and smiled.

"How did you get so wise, Mr. Jared?"

Jared chuckled.

"I don't know about that," he said. "I don't feel very wise." He looked at her for a moment. "I have to confess, Mrs. Darnell, you turned my head when I first saw you."

"Oh, really?"

"Yep. If we were the same age, I would make a move on you, ma'am."

"Why, Mr. Jared, how sweet of you to say that. You have me blushing, sir."

They both laughed.

. . .

Jared sat in the saddle looking down at the Diamond D ranch house. His saddlebags were packed and his bedroll was tied on. It was a lovely spring day for moving on. He hooked his leg around the saddle horn, took out the makings and rolled a cigarette.

He hadn't said goodbye to anyone except Fran. She had taken it quietly, holding it all in. She would cry later, when she was alone. They had gotten too close and that was always a problem for Jared. That made it harder to move on.

As he looked down the slope he saw a tiny dot coming in his direction. At first Jared thought it was one of the ranch hands. It turned out to be Kim Darnell wearing McClain's hat and gunbelt. She was on Wildfire and he had his head. In a few moments she was upon Jared, riding a circle around him. She was crying hard.

"Where the hell are you going?" she said, glaring at him.

"Your mom fired me."

"You lyin' sonofabitch!"

Jared saw that Kim was almost a woman now. Fran could soon let go and hand the reins of the Diamond D over to her and young Ramsey. It would grow and thrive under them. Fran could find a nice companion and go to church on Sundays. Life would be good for her.

"Kiss me before you go," Kim said. "I'll pretend it's McClain."

"No. You should forget him."

"I can't. I tried."

"You will."

"When?" she asked.

"After you and Ramsey get married," Jared said. "You'll be a woman with a life and a purpose then."

She stared hard at him.

"You need to kiss me so I'll have something of you," she said, sobbing.

Jared nudged his horse alongside Wildfire. He kissed her softly on the lips. They held it for a while. She pulled away.

"Now you'll remember me," she said and rode back down the rise toward the ranch house.

Jared's eyes were moist as he watched her become a small, moving dot in the distance again. Finally, he turned his horse.

"Let's go, old pal," he said.

As he rode on, he started to think about McClain and how things had worked out for him.

Fate had handed him a raw deal.

The End

About the Author

As a young boy growing up in the city, R. Annan never passed up a chance to see a Western movie. His heroes were Buck Jones, Johnny Mack Brown, Wild Bill Elliot and John Wayne, to name a few. As an adult, he often wondered where his love of Westerns came from. Perhaps it has something to do with his grandfather, John L. Annan, who was a cowboy from Helena, Montana, in days of old.

A Note from the Author

Thank you for reading my book. If you enjoyed it, would you please consider rating and reviewing it? I'd enjoy your feedback.

Look for other books to appear soon. Thank you!